Also by Maeve Friel

ॐ

Charlie's Story
Distant Voices
The Lantern Moon

The Deerstone

The Deerstone

MAEVE FRIEL

POOLBEG

For Daniel

First published 1992
by Poolbeg Press Ltd
123 Baldoyle Industrial Estate,
Dublin 13, Ireland
This edition published 1996
Reprinted September 1998

© Maeve Friel 1992

The moral right of the author has been asserted.

The Publishers gratefully acknowledge the support of
The Arts Council

A catalogue record for this book is available from the British Library.

ISBN 1 85371 225 6

Cover illustration by Alex Callaway
Cover design by Poolbeg Group Services Ltd
Set by Poolbeg Group Services Ltd in Stone 10/14
Printed by The Guernsey Press Ltd,
Vale, Guernsey, Channel Islands.

About the Author

Maeve Friel was born in Derry, educated in Dublin, and currently lives with her family in Shropshire. Two of her books for children, *The Deerstone* and *Distant Voices*, were published to critical acclaim and shortlisted for the Bisto Book Award and the RAI (Reading Association of Ireland) Book Award. Maeve Friel writes for both children and adults.

Praise for *Distant Voices*

"Rarely in Irish children's writing has the time-slip theme been handled with such assurance."
Children's Books Ireland

"The general tone of displacement and unease suits the subject-matter and its environment, leaving the reader uneasy too."
The Irish Times

৯৩

Praise for *Charlie's Story*

"Friel's language and dialogue are not unlike Anne Fine's: they are loaded with character implications."
Children's Books Ireland

"Disturbing and compelling."
Sunday Independent

CONTENTS

Prologue

One July morning just as the sun was breaking through the night sky the hermit Kevin carefully threw out the rope ladder from the hollowed-out cave where he had slept that night, high above the lake. He moved cautiously, knowing that a misplaced foot could send him crashing to his death on the rocks thirty feet below. Down the knotted rope-steps of the ladder he came, shuddering against the chill wind which stirred up the surface of the great pitch-black lake. "No sign of summer coming yet," he sighed.

At the base of the cliff he fastened the rope-ladder to an overhanging rock to keep it secure for his return. Then, turning to the left, he began to pick his way along the stony path by the lakeside, pausing briefly now and again to catch his breath—for Kevin, already in his seventieth year, was by any reckoning an old man now. The sweet song of a blackbird made him glance up in the direction of the beehive-shaped house on an outcrop of rock above his head—this was Kevin's usual resting-place, a comfortless round cell, its stone walls almost three feet thick though a man could not stand up straight inside. Here in the cell he kept his few possessions, a blanket, a bowl and cup and the few tools he needed to prepare food. The astonishing thing was that Kevin had no need to live like this: years before, he had chosen to leave his family—a wealthy family that enjoyed the rank and privileges of royalty—and had adopted the life of a Christian anchorite, a hermit, dedicated to prayer and fasting in the wilderness of

Glendalough, the Valley of the Two Lakes, in the mountains of Wicklow.

As the years passed other men had followed him to his retreat in the valley as word spread of his devotion and of his strange visions. Reluctantly Kevin agreed to let a number of them stay and found a monastery on the site, with him as their leader. They had built their first church down by the lower lake—to which Kevin was now making his way.

Among the craftsmen engaged in the building of the church was a young stonemason whose wife had given birth a few days earlier to twin boys. Alva, for that was the young woman's name, was scarcely seventeen years old and the birth had been a long and difficult one. Just before evening prayers the night before, she had died. Cronan, the stonemason, was beside himself with grief at the loss of his young wife. Now the fear was that the twin infants would surely die too, if no-one could be found to feed and care for them. Two monks had left the night before in search of a wet-nurse who might foster Cronan's babies—but Glendalough, as we have said, was a remote valley surrounded by dark inhospitable woods and Kevin feared the babies would be dead before help could reach them. That was why he had spent the night alone in the cave above the lake, praying for the soul of Alva and the lives of the two baby boys.

He walked quickly now, out from the dark thickly wooded banks of the upper lake, past the ancient stone fort in the clearing, through the overgrown tangle of brambles and ferns on the slopes of the lower lake until at length he reached the ford near that place where the two rivers met. He sat a moment to rest a while before crossing the stream and entering the new monastic city. A pale watery sun hung low in the sky though there was still a heavy morning mist which might yet turn to rain. Kevin watched as the stonemasons and his brother monks came out of the church on the opposite bank. They were stooped low against the unseasonal weather and held their hooded cloaks tightly around their shoulders.

"Dear God," the hermit prayed, "help Cronan and his sons in their desolation."

At that moment, a shy red deer, a doe, came out from the shadow of the woods behind Kevin. She moved directly to the pile of stones where he was sitting and licked his hand. One of the stones was strangely hollowed out, as if carved by hand, making it look like a low basin. Into this natural bowl the deer left milk enough for two newborn babies' breakfast. The graceful creature stood by the stone, her soft large brown eyes imploring Kevin to understand what she had done.

The children thrived and put on weight. Several times a day the deer came to leave milk in the bowl of the rock until the day, a week after their birth, when the monks returned with a foster-mother for the twins.

Cronan, the mason, gave thanks to the magical property of the stone. He sat on the side of the pile of rocks beside the river and said:

"I, Cronan, bless this stone which has saved my children from certain death. And with the God-given powers vested in me as a worker-of-stone, I name this rock the Deerstone. In the generations to come, it will grant the wishes of any child who comes to it in sorrow and need. And to that end, I here leave my sign."

And when Kevin and his followers looked to see what he had done, they saw the mark of Cronan's fingers embedded in the rock, as clearly visible as if he had just pressed wet sand.

The Deerstone and Cronan's hand are still to be seen in the mountain fastness of the ancient monastic city of Glendalough in the county of Wicklow which is where our story now begins to unfold fifteen hundred years after the birth of Alva's baby boys.

1
Paud

Paud lay stiffly in the long wet grass and listened to the voices of the other children as they moved away from the round tower. One of the group leaders was calling, "Vanessa, Vanessa O'Reilly, will you please keep up with the rest of the party!"

Paud flattened himself against the ground and watched them pass, only three, maybe four metres away from him. The gravestone that he was hiding behind was partly covered with damp, bright-green moss and grey lichens so that it was hard to make out how old it was or read the name of whoever was buried beneath it. There were shiny silvery tracks where a snail had crawled across. A spider was spinning out a web from the top, sometimes hanging motionless, then abruptly falling another few inches on her almost invisible thread. Paud was not altogether sure if he found the spider interesting or disgusting but he didn't dare move away for fear of being spotted.

He smelled the unfamiliar wetness of fern and nettles and old stone, and wished with all his heart that the group would get a move on and leave him alone. He had not wanted to come on this stupid outing to Glendalough and now that they were there, he couldn't understand why anybody would want to visit such a place: there was absolutely nothing to see except a pile of old ruined churches in the middle of a graveyard.

"A day out in a cemetery with a packed lunch! Big deal!" he thought. "And I bet those stupid teachers won't even notice I have gone missing until it's time to go back to the bus."

It still shocked Paud that his parents had made him go through with this summer-camp idea. They had gone off on a sort of business trip to France, leaving him behind with his aunt Helen. They had enrolled him at the camp so that he would be out of her hair during the day. "Look, Paud," his father had said, "the brochure is terrific; there are sports, barbecues, excursions, all sorts of fun. Treasure hunts, mountain bikes—it's not a bit like school. You'll love it!"

But the brochure didn't seem so terrific to Paud. He could see it was a sham from the photographs. It was just like his school prospectus showing all these cheerful people playing tennis or using computers when everyone knew the tennis court was so full of potholes it hadn't been used for hundreds of years and the average first-year had about two minutes hands-on at the computer every term. The camp was bound to be the same, three mountain bikes for everyone to share and horrible cheap, greasy burgers at the barbecues.

Parents were so gullible.

"They just wanted to believe I would have a good time. But I'm not—and I'm not going to either!"

He wiped at his eyes crossly and gingerly raised his head to see if the others had disappeared yet. Beyond the gravestones where he lay, he could see the empty space around the tall grey stone tower. Even that silly fat Vanessa O'Reilly had gone. He waited for a moment while a group of Japanese tourists came noisily into view, all busily clicking away with their cameras, then stood up and rubbed at the knees of his jeans where a wet green stain was already to be seen. Defiantly, he kicked the mossy flat gravestone on which he had been lying.

Now he began to move quickly, stopping only at the sound of voices to hide behind a tall Celtic cross, darting in and out of the gaunt grey shells of the ruined churches, tripping over ancient lintel stones that had long ago fallen to earth, and hauling himself up crumbling walls to look through the tall narrow arched windows. From one such vantage point he was able to see the summer-camp party down by the little stream. They were turning left.

Paud jumped down from the window ledge and headed towards the strange building with the pointed stone roof—the only church that still had a roof, he noticed. All around him were more graves, many of them completely overgrown with brambles and tangles of ivy and heather. Here and there on the more recent graves, people had left round artificial wreaths, gaudily decorated in blue and pink like horrible birthday cakes.

The party of Japanese loomed up at him from among the ruins, still taking photographs of one another and bowing at their guide. Paud could hear her talking: "This remarkable little building is probably over one thousand years old and is known as St Kevin's church, or St Kevin's kitchen, probably because of the odd chimney structure on the roof."

Paud strolled casually past her and pushed through the turnstile in the stone wall beyond the church, coming out beside a little wooden bridge which spanned a shallow brown stream. "Wish I had my fishing-rod," he thought as he hung over the railings of the bridge and watched the waters splashing noisily over the flat brown stones on the river bed.

The stillness of the valley and the melancholy rippling of the water made him feel more depressed and lonely than ever.

"How could they have left me behind? They should have known how much I'd hate this sort of thing. As if I didn't have enough school all year." Paud had been a weekly boarder most of that year and was none too pleased by the change from being a day-boy to boarding. "Dumped, that's what I call it. They don't give two hoots about me."

He turned to look at the sign on the far side of the stream, the place where he had seen the rest of the summer camp turn left. *Priory of St Saviour*, it said. For a fraction of a second, he wondered whether he ought to catch up with them.

Then he saw the Deerstone.

It was just another pile of rocks, scattered higgledy-piggledy on top of one another, but Paud felt someone, something, drawing him closer to it to have a better look. One of the stones was hollowed out in a bowl shape and was full of rain-water. Paud scooped out the water, hoping he might find something in it but it was empty. Perhaps it was an old baptismal font from one of the ruins. It was funny that it was just lying there, getting wrecked. He climbed onto the larger rock next to the hollow one and looked around. Everyone had disappeared, even the tourists with their video cameras. Paud stroked the strange indentations on the side of the stone and placed his fingers in them. "Weird, they look just like finger-marks." A wave of loneliness washed over him again and he cried out loud, "Oh, I wish someone wanted me. And I wish something different would happen!" From somewhere very far away came the sound of hammering and a bell ringing. The sun came out from behind the clouds and caught him in a warm embrace of light, clearing away his black mood.

He sprang down to the ground, slapping his bottom with the back of his hand and whooping. He was a cowboy jumping off his horse. No, he was the first white explorer of a strange new land. He was a traveller in the Middle Ages, daring to go where no person had gone before. He sensed he was on the brink of an adventure. The valley was his territory and he would do as he pleased until it was time to catch the coach back to Dublin. What did he care if he got into trouble for leaving the group—what could they do to punish him? Expel him? He laughed and turned deliberately to the right, taking the Green Road towards the upper lake of Glendalough.

2

Luke

The lake was long and narrow, surrounded on three sides by steep thickly wooded mountains. It was absolutely still, shimmering in the cold hard sunshine. For a few moments Paud was taken aback and stared open-mouthed at its serene beauty—but not for long! It seemed too good an opportunity to miss—with no-one in sight he could easily have a quick swim.

"It's deep and intensely cold and far too dangerous," the group leader, Miss Kelly, had said that morning when she was making all her boring announcements on the coach. "Lakes are very unpredictable places so swimming is absolutely forbidden at all times. Don't even think about it!"

But she would never know, thought Paud.

He pulled off his sneakers and socks, then his shirt and jeans and made a neat pile which he weighed down with the plastic bag which contained his lunch. Helen made a mean lunch, it had to be said, ham sandwiches, a banana, crisps, a carton of orange juice and a couple of small Mars bars. After the swim, he'd have the crisps.

He dipped a toe in the water. That woman was right—it was freezing—but it was too late to chicken out now. He flung his boxers in the direction of the rest of his things and made a long expert dive into the ice-cold water. It folded over him, a strong undertow pulling, dragging him down to the murky floor of the lake. Paud fought against it, struggling to rise again to the surface, spluttering and petrified with the cold. His breath came in short shallow gasps, real panic overtaking him. It was as if some evil force existed in the lake, some trapped beast sucking him down into its watery lair. With a massive effort of will, he struck out in a strong crawl for the shore again, furious at himself for being so stupid. He should never have come here alone—what if he had got cramps and drowned? No-one would ever find him.

As he neared the shore, he stopped to tread water—where were his clothes? Surely he had not swum so far from where he had left them. Everything seemed alien now, unfamiliar. Blinded by tears of rage and shivering with cold, Paud scrambled up on to the rocks to get his bearings.

Behind him, a low voice said,

"Who are you? Where have you come from?"

Paud swung around in alarm. A boy, about the same age as himself, twelve maybe, was sitting a few yards away. He was dressed in a long brown tunic made of rough-looking wool and his blond hair was cut in an unkind round bowl-shape like that of some of the wallies at school.

"Monkstown," Paud answered too quickly. He didn't like being caught off-guard like that—and with no clothes on!

"Are you an apprentice? Is Monks' Town like Glendalough?"

Paud looked at the other boy. This is some weirdo, he was thinking, a culchie for sure.

"No, Monkstown is not like Glendalough—it's part of the city, that's Dublin city of course," he added in a sarcastic voice, in case this weirdo thought he was talking about Cork or somewhere.

"How far is it from here? Do you mean the new abbey in Baltinglass?"

"Look, it has nothing to do with monks. It's about an hour from here, if you must know, probably less if you come by car and not in a stupid bus."

"What is a bus? Is it a type of horse?"

"Are you having me on, or what? I'm off." Paud turned away, spotting his clothes now, less than twenty metres away, but the strange boy followed him at a run.

"What an odd sack you have," he said as Paud picked up the plastic carrier bag. "What is the writing on it?"

"I think you need your head examined. It says whatever it always says on a Superquinn bag. Go away!"

But the boy still stood, staring at him as Paud pulled on his shorts.

"Does Brother Brendan know you are here? Have you come with news for Abbot Laurence?"

"Brother who? Look, are you here with some sort of fancy dress party? What's with the outfit?" Paud pointed at the boy's brown tunic. He was feeling better now that he had some clothes on himself.

"I do not understand," replied the boy. "I am Lugaid, son of Dermot, but here they call me Luke. I am Brother Brendan's pupil. He is teaching me to write."

"Are you at some kind of special school then? Why are you not on holiday? Don't tell me that is the school uniform." Paud laughed.

Luke pointed to the far shore of the lake. "My father has left me here in the care of the monks. Brother Brendan is down there, walking with Fidelmus. They are gathering yarrow to make infusions."

Paud slowly pulled on his jeans and stood up to close the zip. Something about this boy was beginning to make him feel uneasy.

"Do you live with monks all the time? Don't you go home at all?"

"This is my home now, since my father remarried. He lives at Ferns now with his new wife, Mor. She is the step-sister of Laurence, the abbot here, so my father left me with him. Now Laurence is to go to the new cathedral in Dublin so Brendan is my tutor." Luke stopped and bit his lip. "My father will send for me, I'm sure, when I am older and can help him, but now is a bad time for him. He has many enemies. But Dublin is his now." He rubbed a grimy fist under his eyes.

Embarrassed, Paud flopped down onto the ground and began to rummage about in his lunch bag for the crisps. He hated people crying—there was always somebody crying in the dormitory at school—though this guy seemed to have more than enough cause.

Imagine being abandoned like that by his father to live with monks all the time!

"Here, have a bag of crisps. They're salt and vinegar, okay?" He threw the crisps onto Luke's lap. "Go on, open them." Luke picked up the packet of crisps gingerly and examined it, slowly turning it over and over in his hands.

"Are you an Ostman, a foreigner?" he asked finally, watching Paud carefully from beneath his fringe as Paud pulled on his socks and began to lace up his trainers.

Paud stopped. The boy was picking bits of grass from between his toes and had left the crisps untouched on the shingle beside him.

Something strange is going on here, thought Paud, looking around him. Everything looks different. There shouldn't be so many trees and I don't remember seeing those stone beehive things. He started to run back in the direction of the lower lake, staring around him in disbelief as the awful truth began to dawn on him.

"Miss Kelly", he screamed, "where are you? I'm lost." His voice came back at him, ricocheting off the sides of the mountains.

"Tell me who you are. I will help you find the person you were shouting for." The strange boy had been running behind him all the time and had caught up with him.

The two boys stared at one another, their eyes meeting for the first time. Both gave a start of recognition as each saw his own face in the other. Apart from their haircuts, they were the image of one another, as like as identical twins.

"What year is this?" asked Paud.

"It is the year of Our Lord eleven hundred and sixty-two."

"No, no, it isn't," said Paud despairingly, his eyes wide with alarm. He grabbed Luke by the shoulders. "I must get out of here. Help me."

Paud's face had become completely drained of colour. Pale-faced and looking younger than his twelve years, he clung to Luke as the tears streamed down his face.

"How, how can this have happened?" he sobbed.

"Why has it happened?" countered Luke. "God must have sent you here to do something."

"Don't be silly. God has nothing to do with it. I've travelled through time. There must be a logical explanation." Paud had seen programmes on television about time travel; it was probably commoner than people thought. All he had to do was get back in the loop or whatever had caused it and he would be back in his own time again. Oh God, the awfulness of it all. Would he ever escape?

"Well," said Luke doubtfully, "the best thing is to hide somewhere until we know what to do. Fidelmus and Brendan will be coming back this way any time now and they should not see you. They might think you were a spy or a runaway and lock you up." He solemnly handed Paud the carrier bag and the bag of crisps which he had picked up at the lakeside when Paud had run off. "Follow me."

He took off like a hunting dog after a rabbit, up above the shore of the lake, hopping from stone to stone, skilfully avoiding the clumps of heather and high nettles which pricked and stung Paud's arms. They began to climb through the trees on the southern side of the lake, pushing their way clear through the dense undergrowth of holly, ivy and bramble. Startled rabbits bolted from their burrows as the two boys raced past. A wood pigeon crashed noisily from its tree perch, crying alarm. Here and there they had to jump across narrow rivulets of water which splashed down the valley into the lake below. Eventually Luke stopped. They had reached a clearing on a high promontory overlooking the lake. On it stood a solitary monk's cell in the shape of a stone beehive.

"No-one comes here any more. They call it St Kevin's cell—he lived here hundreds of years ago and started the monastery here in Glendalough. We all live down there by the other lake. Can you see where the round tower is?" Luke pointed far in the distance where they could just make out the buildings of the monastic city dominated by the tall round tower where Paud had sneaked away from his summer school group. "There is one church near here, St Reefert's, but nobody goes there until the evening. The abbot likes to make evening devotions there for that is the burial place of his family, the royal clan of the O'Tooles."

"My head hurts," said Paud, throwing himself on the ground next to the beehive. "I'm sorry if I was rude to you before. Sit down beside me and help me figure this out."

"I've been thinking," he said after a few minutes. "I must have changed some time before I went for the swim. I had been sitting on a stone beside the stream just beyond the turnstile in the stone wall and I made a wish. I said something like, I wish someone needed me. I wish something different would happen. I was feeling really bad at the time because my parents have sent me away too, just like yours. Well, not exactly like yours, but they have gone away and left me behind and I hardly ever see them any more."

Luke nodded. "Where were you exactly when you made the wish?"

"At a pile of rocks beside the river. One of the stones is like a bowl. It had water in it."

"And the one beside it has marks, like fingers, on the side?"

"That's it, exactly!" shouted Paud. "You know it too. I was sitting on the one with the fingermarks."

Luke nodded again. "We call that cairn the Deerstone. The old monks say it has magical powers but no-one ever believed them. Malachi, the stonemason—he is the leader of the men who are building the new priory outside the city—told me the story about it, about how the hollow stone saved the lives of twin baby boys. But that happened in the time of St Kevin, ages ago."

"Have you ever made a wish on the Deerstone?"

"Yes, I wished for my father's enemies to be defeated and for him to come and take me home. And I wished for a friend."

"Did your wishes come true?"

"I don't know. I just made the wish this morning."

The boys looked at one another, not knowing what to make of this.

"Come on, Luke, let's get back to the Deerstone and find out if it really has the power. If I make a wish, I probably can get back to my own time." Paud leapt up and started to run down into the woods.

"Stop, wait, Paud, we can't go there now."

Paud stopped running and wheeled around angrily. "Why not?" he demanded.

"It's always crowded around there—if you go anywhere near there dressed like that, you will be seized. They will think you are a foreigner, a spy, maybe the Devil!"

"What do you suggest that I do?"

"I think we'll have to stay hidden until dark. The lay-brothers and the monks spend the day coming and going to the mill and tending the cattle and the pigs down by the lower lake until then. At midday everyone gathers for prayers and that means many people crossing the river near the stones. You see, the abbot is building a new priory down in the woods on the opposite side of the river to the rest of the city and there are many stonemasons and craftsmen working there now. There are more people in Glendalough than ever before."

"But I can't stay hidden all day long. I'll have to chance it." Paud was desperate to get away, so desperate he couldn't even think about how or why such an extraordinary thing had happened to him. He just wanted everything back to normal as fast as possible.

Luke nodded gravely. "I've got an idea. You wait here—I won't be long—hide in the cell if you see or hear people coming. I'll go and find you something ... something less strange to wear. Then you can just walk over to the Deerstone and make your wish." He started to walk away, then added, "Are you hungry? I don't know if I can find any food. I'm always hungry."

Paud grinned. "No problem—I have food, look. Look, Luke—I like the sound of that." He opened his carrier bag and took out the banana and the foil-wrapped packet of sandwiches.

"What is that?" asked Luke, pointing to the banana. "Is that food?" He smelled it doubtfully. "It doesn't look like anything I know. How do you eat this?"

Paud peeled the banana and broke it in two. "Here, try it. It's called a banana."

Luke reached for the fruit and squeezed it between his thumb and forefinger.

"It tastes good. What else have you got?" He looked wistfully at the silver package.

"Go on then, open it."

Luke raised the pack of sandwiches to this nose and gave it a good sniff.

"It smells like meat, I think, but I don't know how to eat it. Is this a skin too?" Paud took back the parcel and unwrapped the silver foil 'skin,' enjoying the other boy's puzzlement. For a moment he had forgotten his awful predicament and was showing off his novelties like a conjurer on television taking surprises out of a top hat: "See, this is just shiny paper. And this is bread, white bread although brown is better for you—and this is cooked ham."

Luke took one of the sandwiches and examined it thoughtfully. "It doesn't look like bread. Our bread is dark. I think I prefer the nabana."

"Banana, you wally!" Paud punched him lightly on the chest.

"What is a wally, Paud?"

"You are a wally," replied Paud, grabbing his new friend and wrestling him to the ground.

At that moment the silence of the valley was shattered by the bells of Glendalough's seven churches, hidden from sight but less than a mile distant, ringing out in loud urgent peals. Luke struggled free from Paud's grasp and jumped to his feet in alarm.

"What is it, Luke? What does all the ringing mean?"

"It means danger, Paud. The city is under attack. It's a raid. Follow me!"

3
The Raid

It was calamitous. The thatched roofs of the small mud-and-wattle houses of the lay monks and their labourers had caught fire. A thick pall of black smoke drifted towards the boys where they crouched behind the dry-stone wall which encircled the holy city. From where they lay they could see a tall gaunt monk, dressed all in black, who was rushing hither and thither issuing orders.

"Water!" he shouted. "Form a chain to bring water from the stream." Monks, old and young, scattered to collect a curious assortment of deep wooden and leather buckets and formed a work-chain, hauling water from the river and passing it along to douse the flaming houses. Now and then the chain would be broken as the fire treacherously changed direction in the wind and blew sparks into the faces and streaming eyes of those nearest the inferno. Other monks ran urgently in pursuit of the frightened fleeing cattle and squealing pigs. And all the time the church bells clanged frantically, creating an awesome din.

"Why are they ringing the bells?" whispered Paud.

"They are hoping that help will come from outside. But the local chief in this district is Macdara..." Luke's voice trailed off.

"But what?"

"Macdara is no friend of my father and so no longer recognises Abbot Laurence as kinsman or as abbot. He doesn't like the way the king and the abbot are changing the old ways of the monastery or the new order of monks that are coming to the new priory. He might even have launched the attack."

"What do the raiders want?"

"Often they come to steal the gold and other treasures: others come to take cattle or sheep and corn but sometimes they do it only to frighten us, maybe to chase the monks away."

"And who is that man?" Paud pointed to the thin monk he had seen organising the fire-fighters.

"That is Brother Brendan, my tutor: he is in charge of the abbey when Laurence is away. Look, Paud, I must go and help. We cannot hide here like timid deer. Put on my robe and join the fire-chain." Paud's eyes opened wide with alarm. "Don't worry. In all this confusion no-one will notice you. I will sneak back to the guest-house there and find more clothes." He reached up and pulled the cucullus over his head. Under it he was wearing another sleeveless tunic, shorter and thinner. "Take off your shoes and other things and hide them here behind the wall. Be quick. The city will be destroyed soon if we don't get the fire out."

"But what if..." Paud looked anxiously at his friend.

"Don't worry. No-one will talk to you—you are just another pair of helping hands. And besides you are in the protection of the Deerstone. Go now! Now!" he commanded as Paud hesitated. Together they jumped up on the wall and leaped over into the blazing disaster zone. Within seconds Luke had disappeared among the throng of rushing people. Paud was alone.

The fire among the outbuildings was still raging as Paud joined the line of young boys near the bank of the river. He began to help to haul the heavy slippery buckets out of the water and pass them along to the older men nearer the fire who, red-faced and sweating, shouted at them to work faster.

In the frenzy of work, no-one paid any attention to another small robed figure joining their ranks to help. The stink of wet, uncured leather buckets, the smoke and the sweet stench of burnt flesh of the animals who had been unable to escape the fire made Paud gag but he forced himself to stay in line, rather than run for the safety of the Deerstone. "I'm doing this for Luke, doing this for Luke," he repeated over and over to himself as he caught hold of each heavy bucket and heaved it into the arms of the young man next to him. The weight of the water and its crude container almost pulled his arms out of their sockets. All around him, sparks were flying and bits of burning thatch were carried off by a capricious wind which seemed to change direction every few minutes. Suddenly there was a shout: the thatched roof of one of the churches had taken light. The chain of weary, sweat-soaked volunteers divided and re-formed, redoubling their efforts now to quench the spreading flames.

Paud could hear the ominous cracking of the wooden roof supports before they finally split, crashing into the church with a horrifying thud. The air was thick with choking smoke and the sense of catastrophe.

Where had Luke gone? Why had he not come back for him? Would he betray him? Worn out with all his exertions in the fire-chain, Paud was close to despair. Home and Dublin seemed utterly beyond his reach. He felt he must surely be doomed to continue to live in this terrifying wild world, or worse, doomed to die there.

At last the fires in the domestic outbuildings were brought under control and Brother Brendan called a halt for the water-carriers. Many of the monks stood dazed and horror-stricken, watching the smouldering remains of their homes and church. Others wandered here and there, absent-mindedly picking up a bucket or a rake or just muttering to themselves. Their faces reminded Paud of faces he had seen on television after air crashes or earthquakes; they had the same dead, empty look of horror and helplessness.

He was thinking he must pull himself together and get to the Deerstone before he was spotted. There was nothing more he could do. If only he could have seen Luke to say goodbye.

"You young scoundrel. I wondered where you had got to when Fidelmus and I returned from the lake and found you had not waited for us as I had ordered. Praise be to God you are safe. Leave your bucket where it is and follow me—I have a task for you."

Paud wheeled around in alarm at being spoken to. It was the tall thin monk, Brother Brendan, the one Luke said was in charge.

"Don't look so terrified," said Brendan. "This is not the first raid we have suffered nor will it be the last. We will build again—it is not as bad as you think, my young lord, and besides, we have had no loss of life."

With a mixture of horror and relief, Paud realised that the monk had mistaken him for Luke. For one wild moment he wondered if he should run for his life, heading for the Deerstone and safety—it was probably only a few hundred yards away—but he had hesitated a second too long.

"Come on, Luke, we are all tired but there is still work to be done. And even the sons of kings must do their share of it." Brendan put an encouraging arm around his shoulder. "I want you to come with me to the scriptorium—God willing, our losses there will not be great. Indeed from what I have heard, these raiders were not at all interested in our valuables. It's a mercy they took no hostages either." Brendan stopped and laid his hand on Paud's grimy cheek. "Abbot Laurence may be right—he fears for your safety now that Dermot has taken Dublin and North Leinster. But Macdara, or whoever was behind this latest attack, will soon learn he has found more than his match in the king. And God, Laurence and myself shall keep you safe."

Paud ran alongside the tall black figure as he hurried past the smoking ruins of the outbuildings and the gaunt grey churches. He seemed to be heading in the direction of the round tower where only a few hours previously Paud had escaped from the summer school excursion. "Please, please," he prayed silently, "let the Deerstone work when I get back to it, but first, please let Luke come and rescue me from this man. And then let Luke be safe from his enemies."

At the round tower, Brendan paused and looked up at the arched doorway set about twelve feet above ground level. It was completely sealed with an immense wooden door. In a language Paud could not understand but supposed to be Latin, the monk shouted a brief command. At once a face appeared at one of the small windows high up on the tower.

Paud could hear running steps on the wooden staircase. The great entrance door creaked open, a hefty rope ladder was thrown down to the ground and a huge robed figure carefully backed out of the tower and climbed down to greet Brendan and his small apprentice.

"Well, Brendan, what damage have we suffered this time? Apart from the fires, of course. We watched your brave efforts helplessly, from our bird's nest view."

"Grave but reparable, Abbot Laurence. The raiders apparently intended only to frighten us. They attacked first at the new priory but did little damage with their slings and axes. There are casualties among the masons and carpenters—no, nothing worse, no deaths—and according to Malachi, the masons themselves inflicted some punishment on the raiders. I fear Macdara will not cease his attacks on us unless you send away the new Augustinian monks and abandon the new church. He will never accept your authority here or king Dermot's rule." He sighed and glanced at Paud. "The raiders came only briefly into the city itself to raise the fire and scatter the animals. As you can see, I have Dermot's son safe and well."

"How many were there?" The abbot patted Paud's head absent-mindedly and turned to Brother Brendan again, his high forehead furrowed with anxiety.

"About ten, I am told, all on horseback. Malachi swears they were all dressed in the manner of Macdara's fighting men."

"And Malachi, you may be sure, is right. It pains me to admit it but Macdara has all the O'Tooles behind him now. They appear to have forgotten that I too belong to the O'Toole family. No help at all came from outside the city in answer to our bells, did you say?"

"I didn't say, Laurence, but you are right. We fought the fires ourselves. The little church of St Kieran has lost its roof but we are not short of wood!" Brendan waved an arm at the trees all around them. "Even the worst fire cannot consume our stone walls and we can roof and roof again."

While the two monks were speaking, Paud had been keeping his head low and avoided looking directly at either man. Looking just like Luke was an amazing coincidence but was it enough to protect him until he could get away? He thought he saw the monks exchange a strange look when they turned their gaze on him. Laurence seemed to raise his eyebrow. Paud's mouth was dry with fear. He could hear his heart thumping wildly.

"The treasury was not broken into but it's possible some gold or altar cloths may be missing from the churches. I have ordered the brothers to check for any losses," Brendan was saying. "Young Luke and I are on our way to the scriptorium now to see if any books have been stolen or damaged. It was by the mercy of God they did not know you were here, Laurence, or your life would have been in great danger."

"God's will be done," replied Laurence gravely. He turned to Paud and spoke to him for the first time. "I shall be seeing your father, my lord the king Dermot, at the Clane synod this week and shall tell him of your security and good health. Have you any message for him?"

Paud gulped and felt sick. "Thank you," he managed to say, "I..." He looked around wildly, his brain churning. What should he do? If he spoke strangely to them, detection was inevitable. As he hesitated, a small black figure crawled out from behind a holly tree and beckoned to him. It was Luke at last!

To Brendan and Laurence's astonishment, Paud suddenly bolted away from them and raced behind the bushes from where they could shortly hear loud melodramatic retching as Paud pretended to be sick.

"You must pardon young Luke," he could hear Brother Brendan saying. "It must be the shock of the raid and all the smoke he has inhaled. But tell his father he is well, a little too quiet and somewhat lonely, but well."

Behind the bushes Luke laughed silently at Paud's improvised escape.

"Stop, Paud, that is enough. You'll really make me sick!"

"Where have you been? I've been having kittens. He thought I was you. I was afraid he would make me read something or make notes—he's going to the scriptorium—I supposed that must have something to do with writing. Luke, I will have to go now. You go back to Brendan in my place and I will make a run for the Deerstone when the coast is clear."

"Paud, don't go so soon! You are my friend, my brother. You look like me. I can see you are sad like me. Stay! We will say you are an orphan. They won't turn you away."

"I can't, Luke. I don't belong here. I have a family, another life. It wouldn't work."

"Luke!" Brother Brendan's voice was sharp. "That is enough. Come out of hiding and come with me."

"Laurence said he was going to see your father—he must be leaving for Dublin too," said Paud.

"Your journey will be faster than his on horseback," smiled Luke. "Thank you for helping with the fire. Can you come back some time?"

A lump came to Paud's throat at the thought of the lonely life Luke must live in this wild comfortless place. They hugged each other awkwardly, embarrassed, then Luke pulled away and, without another word, ran to where Brendan was waiting.

"Here I am, Brother Brendan," Paud could hear him saying. "I am sorry for my ill manners but I suddenly took ill."

"Archbishop Laurence was not well pleased by your demeanour."

Luke smiled up at his tutor. "You are calling him

archbishop already? Tell me about the new cathedral of Christ Church and Dublin. Have you been there? Have you heard of a Monks' Town there?"

"Dublin is a foul and dirty place," replied Brendan, "full of heathens and scoundrels. I would not call it a monks' town. But Laurence will soon put it to rights, I dare say, when he becomes archbishop at the new cathedral. I suppose you have heard that your father has taken the city? The latest news is that the high king of all Ireland, Muircheartach MacLochlainn, has accepted Dermot as king of Dublin and Leinster."

Paud strained to listen to their conversation as they walked away behind the tower to a two-storey rectangular building. "Funny, I don't think that is there any more, not even in ruins." But this was no time for eavesdropping. It was time to leave. He had no idea how many hours had elapsed since he had made his wish. Would there still be time to get to the coach and join the others? Would the magic of the stones that had transported him back in time work in the opposite direction? He must get to the Deerstone, and quickly— but first he had to find the place where he and Luke had hidden his own clothes.

4

Lost and Found

Paud pulled the tunic up above his knees and ran out of cover straight for the wall a short distance behind the tower. The rough stony ground hurt his feet—he was not used to going barefoot—but there was no time for delay. Once over the wall, which here was only about five feet high, he crouched down and traced his way back to the place where he and Luke had hidden his clothes and his lunch bag. All the time he kept as near as possible to the boundary wall in case a lookout in the tower might see him and become suspicious. He could hear the voices of the monks and labourers on the other side of the wall as clearly as if he had been standing next to them. He held his breath and crawled faster. The peculiar stone-roofed church of St Kevin's was just ahead where the wall formed a sharply angled turn. That was where they had stuffed the carrier-bag into the blackberry bushes: from there the Deerstone would be within sight, just across the narrow stream. Paud lay low and began to pull off Luke's scratchy tunic.

A rustling sound a few yards away made him stop and pull it back on again. Who or what was making the noise? Was it a pig, one of the ones that had escaped in all the commotion, snuffling around for food? What if someone had discovered his cache? The alarm was sure to be sounded if anyone had found all his outlandish clothes. Paud inched forward, on all fours, hugging the wall, and peeped around the corner. What he saw made his heart stand still.

Just feet away from where he had put his bag, a crouching figure was rummaging among the blackberry bushes. It was not a monk, or even one of the men who worked with the animals, for he was dressed differently, in rough woollen breeches with a short cloak like a blanket fastened at one shoulder. From under his cloak, the man removed a small bundle and poked it under the hedge, swearing—or so Paud imagined by his bad-tempered tone of voice—as the brambles pricked him. When he was satisfied that his parcel was well hidden the man stood up and turned, looking furtively in all directions. He had one hand to his mouth and was licking the scratches. Paud could clearly see his long red hair, his wide green eyes and, most strikingly, his large teeth and the wide gap between the front ones. All of a sudden he turned on his heel and scaled the wall back into the monastic city.

Paud, frozen to the spot, didn't dare breathe or move a muscle until the sound of his footsteps had faded away...Was the man a thief? What had he been carrying in his bundle? And why had he gone back into the enclosure if he was an enemy of the monks? Paud crept forward, every nerve on edge, every muscle primed for a quick getaway if anyone spotted him. He pulled off the tunic and reached into the bushes, feeling around for his own clothes. His fingers brushed against something hard and rough—the bundle the man had been concealing. At that very moment the church bells began to ring, not in the rapid urgent way they had pealed earlier in the emergency but in slow measured rings. They must be calling the monks to prayer. Paud's heart thumped. His hands were shaking so much he could hardly grip his rucksack when at last he found it. Everything spilled out onto the ground, his clothes, the remains of his lunch, his shoes and socks.

Rapidly he pulled on his jeans and stuffed everything else back into the plastic bag, everything except Luke's tunic which he thrust back into the brambles. As an afterthought, he took out the uneaten ham sandwiches and the chocolate bars and pushed them into the folds of the tunic. He could imagine Luke's face when he came back for it. Hadn't he said he was always hungry?

Then Paud ran, straight as a die for the stream and the Deerstone. Nothing would stop him now!

"Where have you been? Didn't you hear me say the coach was leaving at five o'clock sharp? What on earth do you think you're doing, sitting there, half-dressed, on that pile of stones? Have you been swimming? Is that what you've been doing, you young pup?" An angry hand brusquely grabbed Paud's shoulder and Miss Kelly's indignant voice abruptly brought him back to the twentieth century. "Don't dare say you haven't heard us shouting for you. We've been up and down here at least half a dozen times. Just you wait until I speak to your parents about this."

Behind her the rest of the summer camp children stared at Paud who had materialised so unexpectedly in front of them. They all looked fed up and tired—but most of all relieved that Paud was now the butt of Miss Kelly's hectoring attention: they had all had enough of her bad temper ever since she had noticed that Paud had gone missing. For the past hour they had had to stick together like leeches, never straying from her sight. When Paud hadn't even turned up at the coach park at five o'clock, she had become worse than ever. Until then she had supposed that he had got mixed up with Mr Burke, or Miss Austin's groups but they had all come back on time without Paud. The search parties had been going around in circles for over half an hour.

Paud's lower lip trembled. He had never been so happy to see the dragon Kelly in all his life. His eyes filled with tears.

"Mary, the boy's upset. I'm sure he didn't go astray deliberately. Leave him to me. We'll follow you back to the coach. Come on, lads, the mystery's solved! Back to the bus, everyone." Mr Burke waited as the children filed off after Miss Kelly. As far as they were concerned, the drama *was* over. One or two turned back and jeered at Paud for stirring up so much trouble—they hoped he'd get it for keeping everybody hanging around so late. Paud stood up shakily and threw his arms around an astonished Mr Burke. "I'm so glad to see you, sir."

"Take it easy, Paud. Don't mind Miss Kelly. She was just like that because she was frightened that something might have happened to you. Come on, let's get out of here." He ruffled Paud's hair. "You look as if you've been in the wars. You're filthy—and where are your shoes?"

Paud sat down on the rock again and fished out his T-shirt and socks and sneakers. It was then he felt the sack bundle at the bottom of the carrier-bag amid the debris of lunch things.

"Oh, Luke!" he said hoarsely, colour draining from his face.

"Look at what?" said Mr Burke, bending down.

"Oh, nothing." Paud hastily pulled on his shoes and picked up the bag again, clasping it tightly to his chest.

His brain was churning. What had he taken? What was he going to do about it? In a daze, he followed Mr Burke across the wooden bridge and through the turnstile back into the ruined city of Glendalough. The stone-roofed church of St Kevin looked surprisingly similar but the little church whose thatched roof had fallen in, in the fire, had all but been destroyed by time. The cathedral looked smaller and less imposing than he remembered it but the slender grey round tower was as striking as it had been in Luke's time.

"You know, sir, there used to be a door up there off the ground and the monks could climb up with their treasure during a raid and pull up the ladder behind them and stay safe until the raiders had gone." He felt as if there was a frog in his throat.

"That's right, Paud. It is a fascinating place if you use your imagination. Are you interested in history?"

Paud looked at his hands. The dirt on them was

more than eight hundred years old, the smears of soot from a fire that blazed in a raid in the time of Laurence O'Toole. In his Superquinn carrier, he had a piece of sacking containing heaven knows what. It seemed that history had somehow got interested in him. Most importantly, he now knew that there had been a boy, just like him, who had once lived in Glendalough with the monks and who might even have become a king one day.

He walked alongside Mr Burke out through the arched gateway, leaving the ruins behind.

"Did you notice any of the marvellous carvings on the stones at all, Paud? This one here was the sanctuary cross." The teacher pointed out the faint outlines of a cross carved into a huge rectangular stone slab on the wall of the gateway. "If someone outside the monastery was a refugee, fleeing from punishment say, and managed to make it to this cross, he could claim protection—that is what the word sanctuary means. I'd say that cross could tell a few stories, what?"

Paud stopped on the steps before the entrance and let Mr Burke walk on a few steps. A man had set up a stall and was selling postcards and Aran sweaters and souvenirs for tourists. Opposite at a mobile shop a woman was filling ice-cream cones for a family of noisy children. Two back-packers in yellow anoraks were sitting on the low wall beside the stream, sharing a can of Coke. They all looked so *normal*, so out of place! Paud hugged his bag closely to him and wondered what the bundle contained and what he could do with it. Across the chasm of more than eight hundred years came the magnetic pull of his other-world twin and the mysterious power of the Deerstone. At that moment he knew that he and Luke had awakened a strange and ancient force which could not be ignored. Looking back through the gateway arch into the ancient city, he promised, "If I can, Luke, I will go back!"

5

Secrets

It was a silver cup. It might have been a chalice, like the priests used at Mass at school, though it was far more beautiful than anything he had ever seen them using. It was about nine inches high with a deep wide bowl and a short stem. There were two wide gold bands, heavily inscribed and studded with yellow and green stones, one around the top of the bowl and the other on the base. Paud thought they looked like real jewels but he couldn't be certain. Maybe they were just glass. The silver parts were decorated with elaborate patterns of circles and dots and spirals. There was a cross etched in the front. It looked brand new.

Paud roughly cleared a space on the table in his bedroom, sweeping the half-constructed model plane and the instruction manual to the floor, and carefully placed the silver chalice on it. He needed to think, but the chalice gleamed, blotting out all other thoughts from his mind. The piece of old sack was lying on his bed: for the umpteenth time Paud picked it up and wrapped up the treasure. He could imagine being interviewed on television, his photograph in all the newspapers.

Boy Finds Mediaeval Chalice

Chalice Worth £1 Million, Says Trinity Professor

It could be great being famous; his parents would even have to come home. But what if no-one believed his story? The fact was the truth was unbelievable. He would just have to say he had got separated from the rest of the group, started rummaging around and found the chalice. But where? They would make him go back and show the exact place. Archaeologists were real sticklers for detail, he knew that. There had been a programme on television where they were using egg-spoons to dig with in case they destroyed clues! Everyone would know he was lying—a thing like that could not have been lying around above ground for more than eight hundred years without being wrecked. And the sacking would have fallen apart.

Paud was at a loss to know what was the best thing to say. He could not say he had been digging—there was no hole to show them, no earth on the sack. He didn't have a metal detector (weren't they illegal, anyway?) but no-one would believe he just stumbled over the thing. That was just the beginning. Why hadn't he said anything to Mr Burke? Why had he waited days and days before saying *anything* to *anyone*? Saturday, Sunday, Monday, Tuesday, Wednesday: five days.

He unwrapped the chalice again and ran his fingers around the beautiful gold bands. His head throbbed

with the awfulness of it all. There was no other solution—
he would have to get back to Glendalough now and
dump it for someone else to find. Modern Glendalough.

"What about the Deerstone?" a little voice in his
head insisted. "You can't just chuck national treasures
into some bush. You'll have to take it back to its owners.
It's stolen property, maybe very important. And at the
same time you can find out if Luke is all right."

"No, no, I can't," Paud shouted out loud. "It was all
just a dream or something. There's no such thing as
magic stones."

The chalice gleamed brightly in his hands.

"Oh, help me, someone."

"Paud, is that you shouting? What's the matter?
Why have you locked the door? What's going on in
there?" His aunt Helen rattled at the bedroom door-
knob.

"It's nothing. I must have been singing along with
the Walkman. You know how you never know how
much noise you're making. I'm coming now."

"Well, it didn't sound like singing to me but if you
say so…You've been moping in there all evening. You
should be outside in this weather, playing football and
getting some fresh air."

Paud hastily rewrapped the chalice in the rough jute
cloth and placed it in a box of old *Star Wars* figures at
the back of his wardrobe. It would be safe in there—he
hadn't played with the figures for years and nobody else
was likely to pull them out now.

Helen was waiting on the landing for him, pretending
to sort out a pile of ironing in the airing cupboard. Or

perhaps she really was sorting it out—Paud was feeling so guilty about the chalice, he thought everyone was suspicious of him.

"Goodness, Pádraig, you're looking very hot. I hope you're not sickening for something." She put a cool dry hand on his forehead.

"I'm fine, honest, Helen. By the way, I wish you wouldn't call me Pádraig, nobody else does. Paud's cool."

"Well, if you don't mind sounding like a bean, that's all right by me. Now, go and have a wash, that's a good lad, and then come downstairs to the sitting-room. I'm expecting a call any minute from your mum and dad. They'll want to hear how you're getting on at that summer camp. I won't mention how you got lost in Glendalough and scared the wits out of that poor Miss O'Kelly, if *you* don't."

Paud slunk past her and locked himself in the bathroom. How was he going to speak to his parents? They would know he was up to something. They always did.

6

The Museum

"Mr Burke, where are the excursions to this Saturday?"

"Oh, hallo, young Pádraig. Did you enjoy the bowling?"

"It was all right. Where are you taking us to on Saturday?"

Paud had caught up with Mr Burke as they came out of the bowling alley in Stillorgan the following afternoon. The two coaches were already waiting to return to the summer camp centre at Belfield and the teachers were counting the children as they boarded.

"Fifty-two, fifty-three, O.K. That's my lot. Just a moment, driver." Mr Burke jumped down the steps of the bus. "Paud, you're holding up the other people. Go and get on immediately or you'll be in Miss Kelly's bad books again."

"Please, sir, it's important."

"About Saturday? Brittas beach, I think, if the weather holds and we can have a barbecue. Or the Horse Show.

And maybe Glendalough again for anybody who hasn't been already. Now run along, Paud, for God's sake or she'll have your guts for garters."

Paud strolled across the car park to the other waiting coach. Dave, the driver, and Miss Kelly were standing outside it, consulting a list of names.

"Pádraig Fitzgilbert! I might have known you were the culprit. I really think something will have to be done about your lack of punctuality." Her voice moaned on relentlessly as Paud squeezed his way through the throng to an empty seat at the back.

A boy called Shane who was taking up the whole of the long back seat threw a sweet-wrapper at him. "I'm going to get you, Fitzgilbert. You're annoying me, keeping us all waiting every flipping day."

Paud turned his back on him. Shane was the least of his worries. All he cared about, all he could think about, was making sure he got back to Glendalough. And in the meantime there were so many things he had to find out. The coach sped down the dual carriageway towards Belfield.

After lunch they were supposed to divide into groups for tennis, kite-making or canoeing on the lake. Paud's name was down for kite-making—it had seemed a good idea at the time—but there was no point in wasting any more time. He would have to go on the hop.

"I've just been sick, miss. Is it all right if I go home? I think I might be sick again." Paud, wearing his most hangdog expression—really he deserved an Oscar for these performances—was in the school office. Jackie, the secretary, stopped what she was doing at the computer and turned to look at him doubtfully. "I haven't got anybody to take you home, Paud. We're very short-staffed. Could your mother or somebody come and pick you up?"

"My parents are in France and my aunt Helen doesn't drive. I can take the bus."

"I don't like it, Paud. I tell you what. I'll order a taxi and give your aunt a ring to say you are on the way."

"No, no, don't do that!" Paud suddenly saw himself stuck in bed for the whole afternoon with Helen fussing all over him. It would be even worse than the kite-making. "Oh, oh, I'm going to be sick again." Covering his mouth with both hands, he raced from the office and down the passage in the direction of the washrooms, before Jackie could even get out from behind her desk.

"Oh, well," she said to herself, "there's nothing more I can do until he comes back. Thank goodness he didn't get sick in here."

Paud, meanwhile, had no intention of coming back. He skirted the corner of the administration block and set off purposefully down the avenue to the main road where he could get a bus into the city centre. He could have waited for a bus on the campus but he didn't want any nosy parker asking him where he was going. The place was buzzing with people, the camp students setting up their canoes on the lake, and millions of others criss-crossing between the library and the restaurants.

"I'm getting rather good at this escape lark," Paud grinned as he jauntily set off for the bus stop and flight to the city centre.

Kildare Street was long and narrow and full of shadows after the bright open space of St Stephen's Green. Paud looked for a sign that would say National Museum. At length he came to a run of high railings in front of a large imposing building in a courtyard. A huge burly policeman with bright red cheeks was standing in a sentry-box while another man with very hairy hands operated a barrier, letting cars in and out. "Excuse me," said Paud, "is this the National Museum?"

"Well, son," said the policeman, "a lot of people would say that the folk in here make an exhibition of themselves all the time, but I don't think think that is what you have in mind."

Hairy-hands laughed and said, "That's a right one, Con," and winked at Paud who was feeling sorry he'd bothered to speak to them.

"This is Leinster House, lad, in all its glory," the policeman went on, waving a freckled hand at the buildings behind them. "The Dáil, don't you know?" he added as Paud continued to look puzzled. "But that, over there, is the National Museum—go in that small gate you just passed."

The museum had always seemed a boring sort of place to Paud, somewhere he had been taken to by his mother when his Dad was at rugby internationals or on school outings when no-one seemed to know exactly what they were supposed to be doing. He drifted among the display cases, glancing at the gold torcs, the leather shields of warriors of ancient times, the skeletons found in old passage-graves, old pots, until finally he came face to face with what he had been looking for: the

Ardagh chalice. With a mouth suddenly gone dry, he murmured, "Oh, Luke!" It was almost identical to the one which now lay wrapped up in grimy sacking at the back of his wardrobe.

"It's a magnificent specimen, there's no doubt about it," said a voice behind him.

Paud swung round in alarm to see who had spoken. The museum attendant smiled.

"Did I give you a fright, son?" he said in a broad Dublin accent. "I've been watching you. You look like a young man with a mission. We don't get many young ones in here on their own. I said to myself, Mick, that's a fella that knows what he's after. Are you doing a school project or what? The way you looked at that chalice was a sight for sore eyes, I can tell you. Most young ones would walk right past that, and that's the truth, I'm here to tell you."

Paud improvised. "Yeah, I'm doing a project. Could you give me some information?"

"What exactly would you be interested in, like?" asked the attendant. "Do you want to know who found it, that sort of thing?"

"I really want to know about monasteries and raids and things like that." Paud hesitated. "And if you have ever heard about a king called Dermot or a man called Laurence from Glendalough, that would be great."

"I can see you have been doing a bit of homework. But first let me tell you that this chalice here is not from the twelfth century when your King Dermot was alive— it's earlier than that. But the Laurence you're talking about would be Laurence O'Toole who was abbot of

Glendalough and he became the first Archbishop of Dublin at Christ Church cathedral in or about 1162." As Paud gasped—that was the year Luke said it was—the man continued, "And that's an awful long time ago, as you and I well know. The same Laurence is the patron saint of Dublin but I suppose you know that already?" Paud shook his head.

"Jaysus, sometimes I wonder what they teach you at school these days. You all know everything there is to be known about dinosaurs and Egyptian mummies and divil a thing about your own city."

"I was in Glendalough last week," countered Paud, "and I know trillions of things about that. Did you know that some children my age had to live there with the monks?"

"As a matter of fact I did know that, son. They were sort of fostered out to be educated. By the way, what's your name? Mine's Mick and I'm pleased to meet you." He stuck out his hand.

"Paud—that's what everybody calls me. It's short for Pádraig Fitzgilbert."

"Fitzgilbert, is it? It's no wonder you have an interest in the twelfth century. That's when your ancestors, the Normans, came over, invited as it happens by that same King Dermot Mac Murrough."

Paud's eyes opened wide. "What else do you know about King Dermot?" he prodded.

"Let's see now, what can I tell you about him. Well, Dermot Mac Murrough was the king of Leinster though he wanted to be the high-king of all Ireland. Unfortunately, he wasn't the only one after the job and they were all marching and counter-marching across the country, each trying to seize a bit of power here and a bit of land there. The upshot of the the whole business was that Dermot was sent packing. But off he went to Wales to get help from his Norman friends there. And then didn't he invite a party of Norman soldiers back to Ireland to help him seize the high-king's throne here— and because you don't get help for nothing, he promised them land and titles—because there is no such thing as a free lunch like the man said."

"And did Dermot become the high-king?" interrupted Paud, excited at the thought that he had probably met the son of a high-king of Ireland.

"No, he didn't, Paud, for he died soon after he brought the Normans over. But he did marry off his daughter Aoife to that Strongbow, the leader of the Normans, and so he did change the course of Irish history."

"And when was that? When did the Normans come?"

"In 1169, I believe."

"Seven years later," murmured Paud.

"What was that?"

"Oh, nothing. Look, thanks a million for the history lesson. I'd better be going."

Mick put an arm around Paud's shoulder as they walked back towards the entrance hall.

"History is all very well and good but it won't put hairs on your chest. A lad like you should be out and about in this fine weather."

Paud grinned. "I'm going on a trip tomorrow, a treasure hunt. I'll get all the fresh air I need then."

"See you around son. Take care."

"See you, Mick. I'll be back."

"Make sure you are. I'll be looking out for you."

Paud walked up to Stephen's Green where he sat down on a park bench in front of the lake. A small child was throwing bread to the ducks. A punk with a Mohican haircut and safety pins in his nose was winding tangled tape back into a cassette with a lollipop stick. Paud felt weird, suspended on the threshold of a world where reality and unreality met. He was beginning to feel sure that the magic of the Deerstone had not come to life just by chance. There had to be a reason for it. He would *have* to go back, to return the chalice and to find his twin, Luke. Somehow he had a part to play in the great events that had taken place at that time: whatever the dangers ahead he would trust in the power of the Deerstone to bring him back to safety—but he *had* to go back.

7

Return to Glendalough

A great phalanx of black clouds was advancing down the valley at great speed. A chill wind whistled through the tops of the trees, rustling their leaves. The air sighed and moaned like some great beast waking in a bad temper from a disturbed sleep. Paud imagined the clouds bearing down on the whole country from the northern oceans, blotting out the whole of Ireland beneath a cold damp canopy. He stepped off the Deerstone and shivered as the first drops of rain began to fall. Once again he had unlocked the enormous power of the stone-mason and had stepped back, behind his own time, and now stood in front of the mediaeval monastery in all its strange and wild magnificence.

He moved quickly behind the embankment of earth and stones that circled the main group of buildings and took cover in the brambles and tangled gorse which grew there. This was where he and Luke had hidden before joining in the fire-fighting the week before. He looked at his watch: ten thirty. Only minutes had elapsed since he had escaped the eagle eye of Mr Burke, thanks to that bully Shane Taylor and his gang. Just as they were passing under the arched entrance into the ruins, Paud had deliberately tripped Shane up and had had the satisfaction of seeing him sprawled on the ground. Within seconds a brawl had broken out with feet kicking and fists lashing out, no-one really sure who was fighting who. Some girl had screamed and gone to call the teachers. Amid the general disorder Paud had managed to flee and had reached the Deerstone before Mr Burke had even started to get to the bottom of what had started the fighting.

In the bushes Paud quickly found what he had expected: Luke had not removed the old brown tunic but the food was gone.

"Oh Luke, you're brilliant! You guessed I'd come back."

He stuffed his own clothes into the rucksack he'd brought along and pushed it into the bushes. "Better leave the chalice here too for the moment—at least until I've found Luke." He pulled on the scratchy old monk's robe and stood up. "This thing sure is uncomfortable, and a bit smelly." He wished he could keep on his trainers—going barefoot wasn't as easy as it looked.

Again he looked at his watch: ten forty. Time to get a move on. Only then did he realise what a gaffe he was making. With a sigh of regret, he took off the watch and put it in the toe of one of his shoes. The brambles scratched his hands as he poked the bag into its hiding-place. "OK. Here goes."

He scrambled up onto the wall, finding toe-holds with difficulty in his bare feet and dropped over. The rain was pelting down and a slow rumble of thunder rolled over the valley.

Paud put his head down and ran, planning to take cover again behind St Kevin's church, but a small group of hooded monks rounded the corner just as he did. Ignoring their shouts, he made for the bridge again and the sanctuary of the Deerstone. It was too difficult after all. There was danger everywhere. At any moment he might be caught out and even Luke, the king's son, could not save him. He could never explain himself to these people—they would probably kill him, thinking he was the Devil.

Let anyone who wanted find the chalice. He would just leave it where it was and get back to civilisation.

The braying of a donkey stopped him in his tracks. From the left of the Deerstone came a party of labourers, slapping a poor protesting donkey which was clearly exhausted. It brayed and wheezed and finally stopped behind the pile of rocks. The red-haired man leading the donkey lashed at it, furiously whipping its backside and shouting at it to move along. The poor ass stood stock still, its head hanging, neither looking to left nor right, as the blows rained down on its back.

"Stop that!" roared Paud, rushing towards the man who held the whip. "Can't you see he can't go any further?"

The man wheeled round and caught Paud by the hair.

"And who do you think you are to stop me, you

young pup?" He pulled Paud's face up to meet his gaze. "Ah, it's our young prince. Well, your lordship, I'll have you know your father's new church won't be built in time if this ass won't carry its load of stones. Shall we tell the abbot Laurence that you arrested our work to save an ass's back?"

"Enough, enough, Maeldubh, have some respect for Luke. He means no harm and you were severe on the donkey. Leave it rest a few moments and it will do its share of the work—as we all must." Another man, roughly dressed in coarse brown tunic and sandals, his long fair hair plastered to his head in the heavy rain, came out from behind the cart and stretched out his hands to Paud.

"Well met, Luke. I heard Brendan was keeping you under guard for safety but I was misinformed. We are pleased to see you fit and well, and at liberty. The raids we have had these past weeks must be frightening for you."

"Enough of your genuflections to that young scoundrel," snorted the first man. "Come, Malachi, we have work to do. Leave the princeling to his splashing in the rain. We have more urgent business."

Maeldubh roughly pushed Paud out of his path, making him slip in the ankle-deep mud and stumble onto the rocks of the Deerstone. "Go on, out of my way, or I'll not be afraid to use this on you." He raised his whip and smacked the donkey sharply on its back. It brayed in protest but stepped forward pulling the heavily laden cart behind it. Paud remained where he had fallen, waiting for them to move on.

"Come and see me this evening," the man named Malachi called to him over his shoulder. "Ask Brendan to let you come."

This is an evil place, Paud was thinking. There was no doubt about it—Maeldubh was the man he had seen hiding the chalice in the bushes—but he seemed to be one of the stone-masons. By the way he spoke, he had little time for Luke or for his father the king. There was something about him that made Paud's blood run cold.

He watched the disappearing backs of the two men, then turned to look at the hollow stone of the deerstone and to touch the strange imprint of the five fingers. No, he would not make the wish yet. That donkey-beating sneak was up to no good and Paud would find out why. But the first thing he had to do was to find Luke and let him know.

*

Brother Brendan was vexed, his patience having been tried to breaking-point more than once in the past five days. Young Luke was clearly destined to be a man of action like his father—since the day of the last raid he had talked of nothing else—not at all behaving like the studious young soul he had appeared to be until then. The monk picked up another goose feather and patiently began to shape the quill into a nib. Behind him Luke fidgeted at the window.

They were in the workshop on the ground floor of the scriptorium, the place where the monks copied out manuscripts and designed and wrote their books. Along one wall hung a collection of leather satchels, used to carry the finished books. On another wall there were several calfskins stretched on frames—this was one of the stages in preparing the vellum, which was what the monks used to write on. Brightly coloured bowls of ink stood on the table, golden-yellow, emerald green, red, black and brown. On the table beside Brother Brendan lay a tray of goose feathers, a wooden cutting block and a selection of pen-knives.

The rain, still pelting down outside, seemed to have permeated every stone of the workshop. The walls felt cold and damp to the touch and although it was not yet midday, the room was as dark and dreary as any midwinter afternoon.

"When it stops raining, can we go out for a walk, Brother Brendan?" asked Luke.

"No, we cannot, Luke. You know what Laurence said—you must stay indoors until his return. There are rumours that you might be taken hostage if the raiders come again."

"But why, Brother Brendan? What use would I be?"

"A hostage is always of use—enemies will take hostages to bargain with. Indeed it is well known that a conquered tribe will even give hostages to prove they have submitted."

"You don't mean my father would hand me over to his enemies?"

"Of course not. I only mean your father has made many enemies in these parts and until the matter is solved between him and Macdara it will be wise for you to stay out of sight. I have been told to say that you have been taken to Dublin to see your father for even here in Glendalough we cannot trust everyone. We may have spies in our midst."

"Why should my father have enemies here?"

"Luke, come and sit down here beside me and help me make these pens for the scribes."

Luke reluctantly took the stool beside Brendan and picked up one of the goose quills.

"See how I have already formed the nibs with my pen-knife?" Brendan said, neatly snipping at the tip of the feather. "Now I want you to remove the flights, these feathers," he added as Luke looked at him with a puzzled expression. "Without the feathers they are lighter and cleaner—and besides when they are stripped they can't tickle your nose when you are writing."

He tickled Luke's nose with the feather in his hand.

For a minute or so, Luke worked at snipping off the white feathers from the quill, using one of the short sharp knives, but it was not quite as easy as Brendan made it look. After a while he laid down the knife and said,

"Brother Brendan, talk to me about my father. Do you know I have seen him only once since I was three years old and now I am nearly thirteen? And that was only for a few days last year when he took me from my mother's house and brought me here."

"Luke, you can be proud to be your father's son. Dermot has been a good and popular king in Leinster these past thirty-six years—he came to the throne when he was barely sixteen years of age, not long after your grandfather, rest his soul, was murdered in Dublin by the foreigners there. But this is an age when the whole country of Ireland has seen much bloodshed and strife. Six years ago the most powerful king in Ireland, Turlough O'Connor, died. He had been trying to become the Ard-Rí, the high king of all Ireland, but had never succeeded. For three years after his death the four provinces saw much bloodshed as all the local kings battled for power, each of them hoping to win the supreme prize of the high-kingship. Finally, three years ago, in 1159 after a bloody battle at Ardee, Murtough O'Loughlin from the north, king of the Uí Néill, was recognised as the strongest for the time being—though there is still no high-king as such and until this matter is resolved there will be great internal wars."

"But," interrupted Luke, "isn't Murtough O'Loughlin an ally of my father?"

"Yes, it is true that Dermot has sworn to support O'Loughlin and he, in turn, accepts Dermot's position as king of Leinster. But even though Dermot is in favour with the most powerful king his weakness is here in North Leinster, especially Wicklow, where the local tribes want nobody but themselves to govern."

"Do you mean Macdara and his men?"

"It is hard to explain, Luke. You see, the local tribes who have always ruled in these lands are the O'Tooles and they have elected both their local kings and their abbots from among their own people. Now Dermot who is from the Uí Cinsealaigh has extended his rule to these parts and installed Laurence as the abbot."

"But Laurence is an O'Toole too. Why should Macdara be against him?" asked Luke.

"Because Laurence above all is a priest and a good man. He will put the church before all else and ensure that no future abbot of Glendalough can just 'inherit' his office. In times past the monastery has been controlled by laymen who were not priests or holy men. They took the wealth and income of the churches and had the right to ask for burial fees from the local people. Some of the abbots even married and lived in separate houses with their families—Laurence may be an O'Toole but he is determined to reform the Irish monasteries, bringing in the new orders from Europe. King Dermot is for these reforms too and has given land and wealth to build new abbeys in Baldoyle and Baltinglass and in his own township of Ferns."

"What can Macdara do then?"

"The worst. He probably plans to seize control of Glendalough and thus close off the roads which lead from Dublin south and west to Dermot's home at Ferns. Then, as well as expelling Laurence and taking over the city, he might even be able to topple your father, especially if he joined forces with Tiernan O'Rourke."

"And who is he?"

"Tiernan O'Rourke is a dangerous man, lord of many regions and of none, forever at war with his neighbours. His stronghold is at Daingean Bona Cuilinn in Roscommon but where his borders end, none can say for they advance and retreat with every new day, as he forms pacts or makes new enemies. About ten years ago, your father committed a great misdeed towards Tiernan which he will never forgive. I doubt he shall ever forget the insult."

"My father is in the wrong? How is that?"

Brother Brendan's cheeks blushed with embarrassment. He had forgotten for a moment who he was talking to. "If I tell you, Luke, that it all had to do with Tiernan's wife, Dervorgilla, and reflects no credit on any of the parties, that is enough for you to know." He stood up and walked to the window. "The rain is still coming down in sheets," he said.

Luke sighed. He knew he would get no more information out of Brendan that afternoon. It was always like that. Where women were concerned, the monks just didn't want to know. He couldn't even speak about his own mother, the lady who had been married to Dermot before the king married Mór. He hadn't seen her for more than a year, since the day his father came and took him to Glendalough. Before he left, his mother had promised him it would only be for a short time, that Dermot was showing his good will to the O'Toole lords by leaving his son in their territory. He had probably married Mór O'Toole for the same reason, Luke now suspected, if it was so important to have all the Leinstermen behind him, North and South, from Dublin to Okinselagh, from West Wicklow to the sea. If only he had left Luke out of all his intrigues, safe at home with his mother and his cousins.

Luke walked around the table to Brendan's side. Both of them looked out at the teeming rain, the sombre granite buildings and the dark brooding mountains beyond the enclosure wall. Not a being stirred, the monks all indoors at prayer or in their workshops.

"Brendan," Luke began, "do you believe in magic?"

The monk smiled. "No, Luke, and nor should you. But that is not to say that the Lord does not move at times in mysterious ways…"

"Do you remember the day of the first raid, the day the roof of the church caught fire?" Luke interrupted before Brendan could start another of his little sermons.

"Of course, my boy, it was only eight days ago, God forgive the rogues who…"

"Well," interrupted Luke again, "a strange thing happened to me that day and I think it must be a sign."

"A sign, young man? What sort of sign? What are you talking about?"

"I met a stranger by the lake that day, a boy like me, but he was not from here. He said he had come from another time. He didn't talk like us but I could understand him. He helped put out the fire. Then he disappeared again."

Brendan seized Luke roughly by the shoulder and pulled his face up to look him straight in the eye. "Luke, what is this you are telling me? And why have you delayed so long in telling me of a stranger among us when I have been warning you night and morning of spies and enemies? Come on, out with it. Tell me the whole story."

Luke pulled away and sat down unhappily on the work-bench, fighting to stop the tears which filled his eyes. He should never have started to tell his secret. The boy had been a friend, like a foster-brother, not a *spy*. All week he had been praying for him to come back. He had even gone to the Deerstone and *wished* for him to come back—and now he had given the game away.

Just then a large round stone flew in the open window, landing with a thud among the bowls of powdered inks on the work table and scattering the tray of goose quills onto the floor. Brendan rushed to the window to see who the delinquent was, imagining at the very least one of the juvenile apprentices or, at worst, that another raiding party was about to force their way inside. Luke picked up the stone from among the spilt remains of the inks and the overturned feather pens. Scratched on the stone there was a crude drawing of, what did he call it? A nabana, a banana, that was it! And the letter P for Paud. Luke's heart almost burst with happiness. Paud had come back. He was there in Glendalough. The Deerstone had worked its magic once more.

8
"What trick is this?"

Paud crouched behind the round tower. As he had hoped, his rock missile had brought the monk to the window. He prayed that Luke would pick up the rock and understand the significance of the banana shape scratched onto the surface. If he did, he would surely leave the scriptorium and come looking for him. Paud peeped around the corner. He caught a quick glimpse of Brother Brendan's anxious face at one of the arched windows and hastily withdrew from sight. The rain was still pelting down, stirring the earth into a quagmire of mud. No-one else seemed to be outdoors, not even the labourers who tended the cattle and pigs. How long could he wait, Paud wondered, before he got his death of cold.

A loud bang made his heart jump into his mouth. The door of the scriptorium opened and Brendan came running out, his head covered by his hooded cloak, his back bent against the rain and the wind. Paud flattened himself against the wall and inched cautiously around the tower. The monk hurried past, quite oblivious of Paud's presence, in the direction of the gates.

Paud broke out of cover and ran straight to the shelter of the doorway of the scriptorium. Malachi had said he thought Luke was locked up for safety: Paud had to take the chance that he had been alone with Brendan.

"Luke," he called in a loud whisper. "Luke, it's me, Paud." He knelt down and looked through the keyhole.

Luke was sitting at a low table, apparently alone and sorting a pile of feathers. A sleek well-fed cat, with reddish-brown fur, dozed on the bench beside him. Paud tapped gently on the heavy door. Come on, Luke, why don't you turn around? The cat opened an eye and stretched. "Luke," called Paud again, "turn around, it's me, Paud." The cat lazily stretched again and jumped down to the floor. It walked to the door and mewed. At last, Luke, distracted by the cat, heard Paud's loud whispers and rushed to the door.

"The door is locked. Can you get me out?"

"Is anyone else there with you?"

"No."

"How long have you been in here?"

"Since the night of the fire. There was another raid five days ago. The abbot fears they will take me as hostage. When it is safe to travel, I think they will send me back to my mother and her brother's family. Why did you come back?"

"I need your help, Luke. I found a chalice, gold and silver, in the bushes. I think a man called Maeldubh stole it. Do you know him?"

"He is a stone-mason at the new priory, coarse and bad-tempered, not like my friend Malachi."

"I just saw them both. We need to talk. Where has Brendan gone? When will he be coming back?"

"He has gone to see Brother Fidelmus and to fetch food. He won't be long."

"Then we have no time to waste. Where are the keys?"

"They are not here. Brendan wears them on a belt."

"Then you'll have to get out one of the big windows. Go round to the side. I'll keep watch while you open the shutters."

"No, puss, you must stay indoors. It's too wet for cats." Paud standing at the foot of the window could hear the insistent mewing of the cat and several loud bangs as Luke tugged at the heavy wooden shutters at the window casement. A few anxious moments later, Luke's face appeared at the narrow opening and he dropped heavily onto Paud's shoulders. "Liberty at last. I've been in there for days. Let's get away from here, go somewhere we can talk. Brendan may come at any moment."

The two small robed figures were soon outside the enclosure wall of the monastery. A few cows stood morosely in the shelter of the wall and mooed at them as they passed; otherwise they saw no sign of life.

"Where are you taking me, Luke?" asked Paud. "Can't we get in out of this awful rain? I'm soaked through."

"We're going to the masons' quarters. Malachi will know what to do."

"We can't tell anyone that I'm here." Paud pulled Luke up short. "You said yourself they would think I was a spy."

"Malachi is different. Come on, it's not far."

Paud followed Luke at a run, so wet and cold he could hardly think of the dangers he was letting himself into, let alone how they were going to explain his presence. They were following a path which led them along the river, about half a mile from the rest of the monastic city. As they approached the clearing in the forest where the new priory building was going up, the sound of the stone-masons' hammers and chisels grew louder.

"They are all working indoors today. That will be easier for us. Just keep your hood up and your head down and let me do the talking."

They walked together into the chancel of the new church. The team of masons—about eight, Paud imagined—stood on tall wooden ladders or on platforms high up beneath the barrel-shaped roof. Although the church was lit by a few huge candles, it was difficult at first to make out anything, what with the dust raised by the constant hammering and chiselling and blown about by the biting wind which whistled in at the doors and open windows; as his eyes grew more accustomed to the dimness, Paud could make out the rich design on every arch and pillar—there were two birds with a human face between their beaks, a lion biting its own tail, a boat with mast and sails and the heads of the crew. There were geometric designs and flowers, crosses and stars, rows of little balls that looked like doughnuts.

Everything—the doorways and window arches, the pillars—was carved and ornamented but no two decorations were alike.

Luke went directly to the foot of the ladder standing at the broad archway between the chancel and the main part of the church. Paud noticed he did not shout but tapped one of the rungs of the ladder smartly about four times. Immediately, Malachi, for it was he, glanced down and beamed with delight when he saw Luke. Paud stood back in the shadows.

"Why, Luke, well met again. What can I do for you?"

"Malachi, I need to talk to you about something very important. Where can we go?"

Without another word, Malachi led Luke towards a door in the thick stone walls. Luke turned around and beckoned at Paud to follow. The door opened to reveal a narrow staircase concealed in the wall leading up to a long, low-ceilinged room, empty except for a long wooden table with benches on each side. The remains of a meal of bread and roast meat lay discarded on the table. Malachi pushed some things aside and told the boys to sit down.

"Who have you got there with you, Luke? Is he not going to take off his hood and show his face to me?"

Luke caught Paud's eye. "Do it," he said.

Paud slowly threw back the hood and moved to stand beside Luke. Malachi stared first at one, then the other, a broad smile stretching from ear to ear.

"What trick is this, my young lords? Are you brothers, cousins? I never heard Luke speak of you before this. What name do they call you?"

"He is called Pádraig, but prefers if you call him Paud. He is not my brother, at least not my blood brother. If you want to know more, you must swear you will not tell a soul."

"You know me, Luke. If you say I must not, then I will not."

The strange tale was soon told. What puzzled Malachi most was not the power of the Deerstone that had brought Paud to Glendalough back in time eight hundred years, for he, like all those who worked with stone, believed it possessed a supernatural force. He understood that, however cold and unyielding it might first appear, all stone had life and energy. The mystery of Paud's journey from another time did not really surprise him. Malachi had known about such happenings. Indeed Malachi himself had had dreams and visions of other worlds and had learnt the spells which could be woven into the stones he sculpted. However, he was at a loss to understand the story of Maeldubh hiding a chalice in the bushes.

To be sure, Maeldubh was a difficult man. He was a true North Wicklow man, a kinsman of the local lords of O'Toole, the son of a man who had been blinded on the orders of Dermot many years ago—but could he be a traitor to Abbot Laurence? Was he a thief? Anyway what chalice could the boy be talking about? As far as he knew, no-one had declared a chalice missing—there had been no robbery from the churches or from the chapter-house on the day of the raid.

"I am telling the truth, I promise," said Paud.

Malachi turned to Luke. "Could you fetch the chalice

here for safe-keeping? Then I can decide what our next plan should be. If it is as valuable as you think, lying under a blackberry bush is no place for it!"

"And will you speak to Maeldubh?" asked Paud.

"No, I will not confront him until we know more about this chalice, where it has come from and who owns it."

"Maybe the raiders gave it to him as a reward for helping them."

"These raiding parties are not the usual thieves, the Norsemen and the Foreigners of Dublin who in times past used to come in search of gold and silver. These men come to make the community nervous, to gather information for Dermot and Laurence's enemies. They come to find out if the priory is nearly completed, if the new order of monks are here, if Dermot's plans to inaugurate the priory are known. They don't want sacred books or gold-embossed shrines, nor do they have them to give away."

"Brother Brendan thinks they may be looking for a hostage, maybe me!" Luke interrupted.

Just as he spoke, the door at the top of the staircase burst open and Maeldubh marched in angrily.

"Who are these children and why are they wasting your time? While we choke on dust and get no rest from the pains in our backs and shoulders, you hold court with princes and scholars, is that it?"

Malachi pushed the boys towards the door. "They are going now, Maeldubh. The matter was important, believe me. And remember, I am master here. It is you who should not leave your work without my bidding."

He turned to Paud and Luke who stood at the stairs, heads hanging down respectfully, their hoods once more hiding their features. "Do what we discussed and come back here after evening prayers."

The boys nodded and made to pass Maeldubh who was blocking their path. Luke ducked under his arm and got to the stairs.

"And who do we have here?" sneered Maeldubh, grabbing at Paud's hood and pulling him back. His cold eyes met Paud's. For a second they stared at each other's face.

"To be a king's son can be a dangerous position, so they say. You should keep your wits about you." The words, though spoken in a friendly enough manner, were mocked by the stern unsmiling face of the mason. Paud understood immediately that it was a threat.

"To be sure," said Malachi calmly, putting a strong arm around his shoulders. "Go on with you, Luke, and the blessing of God go with you."

*

"You did it! You fooled Maeldubh! He really thought you were me!" laughed Luke.

They had stopped to catch their breath and were sitting in a small clearing in the dense woods that surrounded the priory. It was a dark and lonely place, silent but for the rustle of the leaves of the tall oak trees and the quiet murmur of water where the two rivers met a few hundred yards away.

"That man is evil," said Paud. "You are not safe with him."

He was remembering the first time he had come to Glendalough and how he had felt a dangerous malevolent force dragging him down to the bottom of the lake when he was swimming. Maeldubh gave out that same dark strength. Paud shuddered and stood up. "Luke," he asked, "how did you know I would come back? You left this scratchy old tunic in the bushes deliberately, didn't you?"

"Yes," agreed Luke, "but I didn't know that you would come back. I just *wished* on the Deerstone that you would and I thought I had better leave you the clothes."

"When did you make the wish?"

"The same afternoon, just a little while after you left, I managed to get away from Brendan at the scriptorium. I waited at the Deerstone wondering if you had already gone. Then I made the wish."

"I know when you did it." Paud remembered the weird feeling he had had as he and Mr O'Kelly were walking out of the gateway of the monastery the previous Saturday, how he had felt Luke calling to him. He had turned and looked back through the arch and promised, "If I can, Luke, I will go back." He shivered again. It was better not to think too hard about that stone. He just hoped it had nothing to do with black magic. If it had the power to do good, maybe it could be used to do evil as well.

"I don't know what all this is about, Luke, but promise me one thing. Wait until I've gone before you give back that chalice to Malachi and never, never wish on the stone again."

As Luke nodded, there was a loud snap in the trees behind them. The boys froze and looked at one another in alarm. Had they been followed? Had someone been listening to them? But they need not have worried. Out of the trees strolled a fallow deer who approached and stopped directly in front of them, her large brown liquid eyes curious and unafraid.

9

"Prepare the Guest-house"

As Brendan hurried back to the scriptorium with his friend Brother Fidelmus, he felt a deep sense of foreboding. Luke's story of having met a strange boy by the lake on the day of the first raid was very disquieting, if it was true. Glendalough was a remote place, far from any other settlement, cut off by the forests and the mountains which surrounded it. The only approach was by the old St Kevin's Road, scarcely more than a rough track which followed the valley of the Glendasan river up through the Wicklow gap to the flat plains of the Curragh.

A shout from the top window of the round tower made both the monks turn around in alarm.

"What is it?" shouted Fidelmus.

"A riding-party is on the road, about ten horses."

"Can you make out who they are? Is it Macdara and his men?"

"No, not yet, but I can tell you it's not Macdara. I

believe I can see our abbot Laurence at the rear, in any case it's a man dressed in black and riding a white horse. And one of the riders is holding a child on the saddle before him. They're travelling fast. They'll be at the gates in a few minutes."

"Ring the bells, Felim, to warn the others. Fidelmus, tell Brother Anselm in the guest-house to be prepared for visitors." Brendan agitatedly fumbled for the key to the scriptorium. If Abbot Laurence was arriving with a party—and it certainly sounded like him—there was only one explanation: King Dermot himself was about to visit Glendalough. Brendan would have to put off his talk with Luke for the moment—but, above all, he must ask him not to speak of the strange boy to his father.

He turned the heavy lock and pushed open the door. The cat sprang down from the table and rubbed itself against his legs, miaowing plaintively. "Luke!" called Brendan. "Where are you?"

He ran over to the stairs and took them three steps at a time up to the upper writing-room. It too was empty, the writing-desks at each window cleared, the shutters fastened.

Holy God, where can he have got to? thought Brendan. Of all days too, to choose to play hiding games. He should have known better than to leave him, even for—how long had it been? Twenty minutes, no more than half an hour.

Downstairs again, he slowly looked around the work-room, hoping to detect the slightest movement or noise that would tell him where Luke was hiding. The shutter of the back window was swinging open—

with dismay, Brother Brendan realised that the rascal must have been able to squeeze his way through the narrow opening. Well, he must be found and fast, before anyone asked about him.

From outside came the noise of horses' hooves clattering onto the stone flags outside the gateway.

"Are you all deaf and blind in there?" a deep voice cried. "We are all soaked to the bones and have empty bellies. Will no-one come and offer us some monkish hospitality?" A babble of voices responded in greeting. There was no mistaking that huge powerful voice. It was the scholar Maurice Regan, king Dermot's latimer and master of his household. It was just as he had thought: the king had come to Glendalough!

Brendan left the writing-room at a run and arrived breathless at the gates of the monastery a few moments later. The king's party had already dismounted and the horses were being led to the stables. Abbot Laurence was issuing directions to all and sundry. The master of the guest-house, Anselm, was speaking to Maurice Regan, organising how best to accommodate the whole party which numbered ten men in all: a company of seven soldiers with their captain besides the king and Regan. A small girl, about seven or eight years old, sat by herself on the river bank, forgotten by everyone in the confusion of their arrival.

Brendan approached King Dermot and greeted him with a low bow.

"It is a great honour to welcome you to Glendalough, Your Majesty."

"Why, thank you, Brother Brendan. It is a pleasure

for us to stop and take our rest here. But where is my son? Is he too busy to come and kiss his father?"

"He will be here directly, sire. He may not yet know of your arrival."

"Not know of my arrival? Has Abbot Laurence not told me an hour ago that Luke has been under your personal supervision since the attack eight days ago? How is it that you can know of my arrival and he does not?" The king's voice rose rapidly in anger. He was a large man, tall and stout, with a reputation for being quick to anger. The abbot Laurence, hearing his raised voice, hurried over, his face clouding over in dismay. Trouble already and the king scarcely five minutes in Glendalough. Maurice Regan, the king's right-hand man, was close on his heels.

"Sire, what can I do to be of assistance? Is there something or someone who has displeased you?"

The king held Laurence's gaze for a few seconds. Everyone had frozen, the stable-hands in the act of unsaddling the horses, the monks who had come to assist the travellers to the guest-house, the little girl sitting on the rock on the river bank. It was plain that Dermot was a man whose temper was much feared.

"No, no, Laurence, it is nothing at all. We are just weary from the journey. Let us all proceed at once to take our breakfast for we are sorely in need of it." The king's temper seemed to vanish as quickly as it had risen, as he slapped Laurence on the back and let out a great roar of laughter.

"Come, Aoife, come and I'll carry you through the gates. Then maybe you will be able to see your step-brother." The little girl ran to the king who hoisted her high on his shoulders.

Laurence raised an eyebrow at Brendan who hung back to speak to him. The others moved towards the guest-house with Anselm, nervously laughing, leading the way.

"What did you say to anger the king? Don't you know we must guard against his fury? He is worse than a wild beast when enraged."

"He asked for Luke."

"And why has Luke not come to greet him? Were you not with him?"

"Abbot Laurence, forgive me, I have been very careless."

Brendan quickly recounted how he had left Luke alone when he went to speak to Fidelmus and how Luke had escaped through the narrow window of the writing-room.

"Escaped?" Laurence's voice rose in alarm. "Escaped or taken?"

"He was bored, Abbot Laurence, he will just have gone as a prank. The last week has been hard on him. If only we had known the king was about to appear."

The abbot caught Brendan's arm in a tight grip. "Find him and bring him to the guest-house. Immediately. In the meantime we will keep the king and his men fed and entertained." He hurried off to catch up with the rest of the party.

Brendan, his elderly face pinched with worry, hesitated for a second. Malachi, he thought, Malachi would know where the young prince was likely to be hiding.

Maeldubh struck his thumb nail with his hammer as Brother Brendan rushed into the priory shouting for Malachi to come at once. "May the devil of the lake haunt you," he shouted aloud, pressing his hand under his arm, "can we not get on with our work without these incessant interruptions and clanging of bells!" As he looked down and recognised Brendan, his manner changed. "Oh it is yourself, Brendan, God be with you."

"And with you, Maeldubh," shouted Brendan at the foot of the ladder. "Is Malachi here? I need his help. You have not seen my apprentice, young Luke, by chance?"

"Indeed, I have, not half an hour ago. He was here with a young friend, wasting Malachi's time."

"Is he still here? Where is Malachi?"

"How should I know? Isn't he the master mason?" Maeldubh sneered unattractively at Brendan as he spoke.

As Brendan turned to leave, one of the younger masons called out to him, "Brother Brendan. Malachi has gone to fetch new hammers from the metal-workshop."

"Thank you," Brendan shouted over his shoulder. "God bless you."

"Brother Brendan," called the young man again. "Why were the bells ringing just now?"

"We have visitors. King Dermot has arrived with some of his household and Abbot Laurence from Dublin."

At this news, a strange look stole over Maeldubh's

face. So the King was come at last to Glendalough! There were one or two who would pay him well for that information.

High on a spur of rock above the upper lake, Paud and Luke looked down towards the monastic city, almost all its buildings but the tall round tower hidden from view by the thick forests all around.

"Listen, Paud, something is happening. Those bells are not for prayers."

"Could it mean another raid?" asked Paud apprehensively.

"No, alarm bells are different. I think they mean visitors, important visitors. That group of riders that we saw coming down the mountain must have stopped."

"Do you want to go back?"

"I think I had better, but you stay here. Brendan will be looking for me. When I know it's safe, I'll come and take you to Malachi again."

"Luke…" Paud was reluctant to be left alone as he had been before.

"Don't worry! I will be back as soon as I can."

Paud watched his friend descend the hillside, admiring how quickly he moved despite being barefoot. From bitter experience, he was beginning to realise it was far more difficult than it looked. He could feel the blisters forming already on the soles of his feet and he was bruised and scratched from knocking against rocks and brambles. As Luke disappeared from view, Paud turned to go deeper into the woods to find a hiding-place. Suddenly there was a muffled shout from down below.

"Luke," he shouted. "Are you OK?"

There was no answer but the sound of the wind whistling through the trees. Paud crawled to the edge of the cliff face and lay down, straining to see what was happening down below. He could see there was some sort of commotion in the woods. Branches were shaking. A horse whinnied. There were more muffled screams.

Suddenly out of the trees came a horse and rider, racing at full gallop around the perimeter of the lake, heading in the direction of the road which led out of the valley, up through the dark brooding forests. Paud gasped in horror. The rider was holding a small robed figure in front of him. Luke had been snatched and there was no mistaking his kidnapper. Paud recognised only too well that long red hair. It was Maeldubh, the stone-mason.

10

An Audience with the King

The king was in no mood for excuses.

"What do you mean, nowhere to be found? Did you not promise to foster my son for me, to educate him and keep him from harm?" As Dermot's voice rose in anger, Brother Brendan backed nervously towards the door of the guest-house. Maurice Regan caught his eye and froze him to the spot. Though he had said not a single word, his intention was clear: neither Brendan nor anybody else was leaving until the king had a full explanation for his son's disappearance.

"Calm yourself, sire," said Abbot Laurence, coming to the table and refilling the glasses from the jug of best French wine. "The boy has just wandered off, bored by the enforced stay indoors for the past few days. He will be back by lunch-time, I dare say."

"Well, my good Laurence, I commend your optimism—but how do you explain the fact that every monk, mason and labourer in the valley, even the local cats, has learned that I am here and has come to pay his respects or, at the very least, to satisfy his curiosity? How then has my own son failed to hear the commotion of the horses on the road and the visitors' bells clanging? Is he so blind or so removed from the real world that he does not see and hear monks and servants running hither and thither, carrying squawking chickens and pitchers of wine, preparing clean straw for bedding and all the other requirements of my retinue?"

"Sire, the valley is large and full of hiding-places for someone who does not want to be found," Laurence began.

"No, no, no," shouted the king, thumping his fist on the table. "You are talking of my son, not a common runaway, skulking in the forest for fear of a beating. Why would a king's son run away when he had just given his solemn promise to his tutor that he would wait for him in the scriptorium?" He stopped abruptly and swung around to face Brendan who stood, white-faced and dry-mouthed, twisting his cord belt around his fingers.

"Unless of course his tutor is not telling us the whole truth. Could this be the explanation? Could this supposedly holy man be behind some devilish plan to take Luke hostage?"

"Come, come, Dermot, Brendan is an honourable monk and a most loyal subject of the king." Maurice Regan got up from his place at the table and walked to Brendan's side. "And, I am sure, he has told us the whole truth, have you not?" He drew up before Brendan and looked the elderly monk directly in the eyes.

Brother Brendan shot a look of appeal towards

Laurence but the abbot gave him no sign.

"There was just one thing," stammered Brendan, "but I really don't know if it was just Luke's childish invention—I beg your pardon, sire, but Luke liked to tell tales—perhaps it was true, it sounded strange, but then curious things happen and ..."

"Get on with it, man," exploded the king. "If you have something to tell us, then delay no breath further."

"Yes, sire, I'm sorry, sire. It was something Luke told me just before I left him. He said he had met a boy from another time, that's how he described him, a boy who was like his twin."

"A twin? The boy has no twin. Explain yourself better." Maurice Regan's face darkened with anger. It was as bad as he had feared. The king's enemies had surely got a hand in the boy's disappearance.

Brendan, beside himself with worry for Luke and fearful too for his own safety, managed to spill out the whole story, or at least that part of it that Luke had told him, of how he had met Paud the day of the first raid and how Paud had helped put out the fire.

"He said the stranger was not a spy, neither an enemy of the church nor of the king."

Tears streamed down Brendan's face but Dermot's sympathy was not so easily won. The king turned his back on him and glared at Abbot Laurence. "Forgive me, Laurence, if I am mistaken, but am I to understand that my son, placed in your hands for fostering and safekeeping, has leave to freely wander about this land, these dark lakes and forests, alone? Can you tell me how it should come about that he was unaccompanied and alone up by the top lake?"

Dermot's voice, low and controlled, seemed even more menacing than when he had been bellowing like a lion.

Laurence bowed at the king. "With your permission, sire, I shall send Brother Brendan to form a search party immediately. Then you and I can talk. Brother Brendan, go at once. Take as many men as you like, including the masons and farm-labourers, and bring Luke here without delay when you have found him. Go with God."

Brendan wasted no time in leaving the room, with but a hasty bow towards the king and a sign of the cross. Once he was safely out from under the gaze of King Dermot and his stern companion Maurice Regan, he could think more calmly. He despatched the search party in all directions with strict orders to report back to the guest-house within the hour. He himself took the Green Road towards the new priory: Malachi would be back by now. It was becoming more and more important to talk to him and get his help in finding the boy.

11
Grave News

Paud too was on his way to the priory to look for
Malachi and tell him the dreadful news of Luke's
abduction. It was the most difficult decision of his life:
as he had passed near the Deerstone it had struck him
that he could wish himself out of the whole awful mess
and rejoin the summer-school group. Instead, here he
was, about to break the news that Luke, the king's son,
had been kidnapped by that red-haired gurrier. The guy
was probably in the pay of the local chief, Macdara, the
one who was behind all the raids on the monastery. It
was hard to know why he had chosen that day to take
Luke. Perhaps he had followed them when they left
Malachi and went up to the upper lake. Or maybe it had
something to do with the visitors he and Luke had seen
approaching Glendalough from the mountain road.
The little city had looked very busy as he had skirted it—
something was definitely up. There were people moving
around everywhere where usually it was so quiet. He

had been quite worried that he might be spotted and once or twice had had to take cover among the trees and stand stock-still until the danger passed.

Paud held his hood tightly under his chin and walked directly into the dust-filled church, which still echoed to the sound of the masons' hammers and chisels, and over to the ladder where Luke had earlier attracted Malachi's attention by knocking on the wooden rungs.

"Back so soon? What is it, Luke? I've so much to get through before your father comes to look at the church. And now, of all days, Maeldubh seems to have disappeared." Malachi stuck his hammer in the leather belt around his waist and climbed down the ladder. "How is the king? I saw the party arrive a while back."

Paud's mouth dropped open in disbelief. "The king is here in Glendalough?" he asked.

"You must be the last to know. Where have you been with the other boy? Your father will be angry that you have not gone to welcome him."

Paud tugged at Malachi's sleeve. "Come outside for a moment. I have something to tell you."

"Luke, I'm very busy. Can't it wait?"

"No," replied Paud with such conviction that Malachi gave up all further protest and followed him to the grassy slope outside the stone wall which circled the church.

"First of all," began Paud, "I'm not Luke. I'm Paud." Malachi gave a great guffaw of laughter at how he had been taken in but Paud held up a hand to stop him and went on. "Promise me first by the power of the Deerstone that you will do nothing to put my life in danger."

Malachi nodded. "I promise."

"Luke has been taken hostage. I think it was Maeldubh, that man with the red hair who was beating the donkey this morning. He was riding a horse and he grabbed Luke and they galloped away up the road out of the valley."

"But how did this happen? Where were you?"

"I was up by the beehive cell above the lake. Luke was going back to see who the visitors were. We heard the bells and he thought it must be someone important. Anyway he knew Brother Brendan would be looking for him."

At that very moment the figure of Brother Brendan came running down the path through the trees.

"Luke," he shouted, "thanks be to God I've found you."

Paud and Malachi leapt to their feet in alarm. Paud's instinct was to flee but Malachi put a restraining hand on his shoulder.

"God's blessings upon you, Brendan. What news have you of the king?" he said calmly.

"News of the king? Well, if I were to tell you the truth, I should say that even as we speak he is pacing the guest-house like a caged wolf, that his roar is like the north wind, that I shudder at the flashing of his green eyes, that he is in every respect a king and moreover a man who should not be crossed."

"And what has put him in such evil temper?" asked Malachi.

"Why, none other than this young rascal who

escaped from my care as soon as my back was turned, after promising faithfully to wait for my return. And then, to make matters worse, plays cat-and-mouse, hiding and darting about this past hour, ignoring the church bells, the messages I left here ..."

"What message? When were you here?" interrupted Malachi.

"When you were fetching hammers from the workshop. I came in search of you just after the king had arrived when I discovered Luke had gone. I told Maeldubh the king was come to Glendalough and ..."

"How long ago was this?"

"An hour perhaps. What does it matter now? Let me take this young scoundrel to his father before anyone comes to harm for even Laurence is hard-pressed to keep a rein on the king's temper."

Malachi tightened his grip on Paud's arm. "Brother Brendan, this is not your apprentice. This is not the king's son."

"What game is this, Malachi? Of course it is Luke. I know his face as well as I know my own."

All this time, Paud had stayed absolutely silent, his mind racing from one idea to another. So Maeldubh had known the king was in Glendalough when he snatched Luke! What kind of ransom would he demand? Was he acting for himself or for the local chief? And what if the king couldn't care less that Luke was a hostage? He didn't sound like the kind of man who would make a deal. For all Paud knew, he might be prepared to sacrifice his own son rather than give in to Macdara.

Malachi's strong grip on his arm reminded him of the personal danger he was in too: if anyone suspected that he might be involved in the kidnapping or in the conspiracy against the king, he might never get out of Glendalough, dead or alive.

"...very grave has happened," Malachi was saying. "This young boy will tell you but you must first give your word that you will not let him come to any harm. He has unlocked the powers of the Deerstone and come to us from across the boundary of time. He is here to help Luke."

"But this is Devil's work," cried the monk, blessing himself with the sign of the cross and moving several steps back from Paud.

"No, Brendan, the spell cast on the Deerstone was a good one, made hundreds of years ago to help children in need. If Paud has come here by its power, we can be sure the Devil and his black arts have nothing to do with it."

Brendan was still staring at Paud, shaking his head in disbelief that this figure, this likeness of his young charge, the prince, was in fact a monster, a creature from another world, perhaps the very embodiment of evil.

"Where is our own Luke? What has he done with him?" he stammered at last.

Then Paud spoke.

"Brother Brendan, you must believe me. Luke is my friend. You must help to find him." The monk shrank back another couple of steps, his old lined face suddenly drained of all colour as if he had seen a ghost—which, in a way, he had—but Paud went on. "We were together up by the other lake. We heard the bells ringing so Luke decided to go back to see who had come. He knew you would be angry with him for leaving anyway. Somewhere in the forest below me, he was seized by Maeldubh and carried away on horseback."

"Maeldubh? The mason here? Why would Maeldubh do such a thing?" Brendan turned to Malachi.

"Maeldubh is kin of Macdara. You say you had told him that the king was in Glendalough. I know no more than that."

"Yes, we do," Paud broke in. "We know about the chalice that I saw him hiding last week."

"A chalice? What is the child talking about? What chalice?"

"If you come with me, I will show it to you."

The two men looked at one another.

Malachi nodded. "Come, Brendan, let us go quickly and see what the boy has. Then we will break the unhappy news of Luke and find out what the king proposes to do."

12

Telling Tales

Paud strode out in front of the two men, taking the most direct path along the Green Road and past the Deerstone. For the first time he had no need to skulk in the edge of the woods or crawl around in the shadows of the monastic city's walls. In silence they crossed the river and grimly walked towards the place where he had once again hidden the silver chalice among the brambles.

Paud retrieved the back-pack and, while the monk and the mason looked on with flabbergasted expressions, pulled out his trainers, his jeans, his lunch pack, and finally the chalice still wrapped in the rough jute sacking in which he had found it the week before. He handed it to Brendan, saying, "You unwrap it and tell me if you have ever seen it before."

Brendan gingerly accepted the parcel and slowly removed the sack. As the splendid chalice was revealed, both men gasped.

"Do you know anything of it, Brother?" asked Malachi.

"I do, Malachi. It was the main chalice we used in the cathedral church of St Peter and Paul until it disappeared some months ago. We thought the Norsemen of Dublin were behind the theft. As you know, Glendalough has often been besieged by them. They have plundered our gold and silver plate, and purloined all manner of relics and shrines, valuable beyond description, from the scriptorium. When the chalice was found to be missing, we presumed a thieving Norseman had taken it. But now..." Brendan looked up the valley to the mountains where the chieftain Macdara lived. "This chalice," he went on, "had been a gift to the monks of Glendalough from Murchad, one of the O'Toole kings many years ago. I have even heard it said that he used to carry it into battle as a talisman. When he died, the chalice came as a gift to the abbot of Glendalough along with other treasures of the king. Macdara has always claimed it belonged to the leader of the O'Toole warriors and that Murchad had no right to give it away."

"But did you not think that Macdara might have been behind the theft?" Malachi asked. "Do you think it has been hidden here in Glendalough these last three months?"

Brother Brendan ignored the questions but turned gravely to Paud. "I know not who you are, nor where you have come from. Your speech is not like ours, yet I seem to understand you. You have strange things in your possession which perplex me, bags and boxes in colours and materials I have never seen before—but I do not think this is a trick. I thank you from the bottom of my heart for the return of our chalice."

"Now if you believe me, you must also believe I am telling you the truth about Luke. He has been kidnapped! I saw it with my own eyes. We must do something to save him before ... before anything happens to him." The thought of what might happen to Luke in the hands of his kidnappers was too horrible to think about. Already too much time had passed.

"The boy is right. Come, Malachi, let us take him and this chalice to the guest-house and tell our strange tale to Abbot Laurence and my lord, the good King Dermot. Let them decide what is the best action to take. Macdara, if it is really he who has had Luke taken hostage, will soon send word." Brendan made as if to move away but Malachi stopped him.

"No, no-one else must know about the boy, at least not yet."

"Why not?" demanded Paud.

Malachi paused. The matter of Maeldubh had to be resolved. Had he stolen the chalice from the monks, intending to sell it? Or was he really a spy, working with Macdara to sabotage the monastery? "Would you do something very brave to help Luke?" he said eventually.

"I would," replied Paud, without hesitating. "What do you want me to do?"

Malachi bent down and whispered something in Paud's ear. He smiled and nodded.

"Brendan," said Malachi, " I have an idea."

Aoife, the king's small daughter, sitting forgotten at the window-seat, eating newly baked bread spread with honey, was the first to see Malachi coming running at full stretch towards the guest-house. She turned to Maurice Regan, the head of her father's household, and announced, "Someone is coming with news." Immediately Dermot and Laurence moved towards the arched doorway and pulled open the heavy black oak door just as Malachi arrived, out of breath.

"Good-day to you, King Dermot. We are honoured to have you visit us here in Glendalough." He bowed deeply and went down on one knee before Dermot.

"Who is this?" asked the king, rounding on Laurence, and ignoring Malachi's greetings. "Does he have news of Luke?"

"This is Malachi, our master mason at the new priory. He is the finest sculptor of stone in Leinster and besides, he draws the clearest sketches for the other masons and labourers to follow, he erects the safest scaffolding, he leads his men with charity and yet with firmness and discipline. We are fortunate to have him and his skills. Stand up, Malachi, and tell us what brings you here in such distress." He took Malachi by the hand and pulled him in towards the great stone fire-place where a large log fire burnt brightly.

"Well, Malachi," said the king, "you have no need of further praise from me if what Archbishop O'Toole here says is true. But out with your news, man, if you have your breath."

"We have found your son, Luke..."

"Luke, where is he?"

"There has been an accident. He was lying near the wall, just beyond the river."

"How is he hurt?" interrupted Maurice Regan.

"A blow to the head, I believe. There is no blood but he had lost consciousness and is still confused."

"Let us go at once. Lead the way." The king pushed his way past Laurence and Maurice and seized Malachi by the arm. "Has he said how he was hurt? Did he fall from the wall or is there a felon behind this affair?"

"Sire, I did not wait to cross-examine him. Brothers Brendan and Fidelmus are attending to him. If Your Majesty pleases to come, this way."

Malachi led the king and all the others following behind in brisk procession through the monastic city and out across the wicker bridge over the noisy rain-swollen stream. A warm sun had broken through the blanket of cloud so that they seemed to walk through a fine steamy haze as the heat evaporated the earlier rain.

The Deerstone shimmered in a white misty pool of light, radiating its strength to Malachi, or so it seemed to him as he passed. He had no doubt now that the strange boy who had so unexpectedly appeared was a force for good. The magic power of the stone could only be called upon, it was said, by children in need. At first, Malachi had wondered how Paud's needs could be met by moving back in time to the old city of Glendalough but now he understood: it must have been Luke who had first summoned the ancient blessing of the Deerstone. Paud had been sent to the aid of Luke through the powerful intercession of the magic of the stone. What he and Paud were about to do was full of risk but he felt emboldened by the sight of the Deerstone. He felt stirring within him the ancient and mysterious powers that had been bestowed on him as a master carver of stone. He was sure that together he and the boy from the future would find the means of rescuing the king's son. If that led to uncovering the mystery of the stolen chalice and Macdara's downfall, they might even succeed in bringing peace to the valley of the two lakes.

"This way," he cried, pointing to where they could now see the stooped backs of the two monks Brendan and Fidelmus bending over the smaller figure of a boy lying on the ground.

Paud heard Malachi's shout and groaned aloud. Now came the real test of the protective power of the Deerstone: if it failed, it meant certain death as a devil or a spy.

He watched with awe as Dermot approached. The king was a tall man, at least six feet in height. He had proper regal stature, tall and proud and erect, and walked with the grace of an athlete even though he was somewhat stout. His hair was as black as a raven and was brushed off his forehead in a long black mane while his beard, black too but flecked with grey, was worn long and sleek and parted in the middle. He was, Paud guessed, about fifty years old, a huge, handsome, wild Irish chief, the like of which he had never seen before, not even in history books. He wore a long-sleeved cloak which had once been white, its hem and borders embroidered in red and green and gold. Around his waist he had a wide leather belt with a huge ornate gold buckle in the shape of a hunting dog and from his side hung a short sword in a silver scabbard.

When he saw the boy raise himself on to his elbows, Dermot gave a great roar of laughter and broke into a run towards him.

"How now then, Luke, no broken back after all? Will we live to see another morning?" He knelt down and planted a great kiss on his forehead. Paud noticed he smelt of horses. "Come, Luke, can you walk? Tell us your sorry tale, but tell us first that you will live, before Brother Brendan shakes himself to death from worrying about you. You have been the cause of much worry this morning." The king gave a great roar of laughter and slapped Brendan enthusiastically on the back, almost knocking the monk over.

Paud sat up and allowed himself to be pulled to his feet. "I am happy to see you, father," he said in a small low voice.

"And I am happy to see you too, my son, after all these months. Have you grown?" He pushed Paud away an arm's length and looked hard at him. Out of the corner of his eye, Paud could see Brendan turn pale and clutch at the wooden cross he wore around his neck. "Why, Luke, you have grown three years in one! Is he not, Maurice, the very image of his father?"

"Aye, that he is," agreed Maurice Regan, stepping forward. "But let us hear what misadventure has befallen him."

Paud slowly let out his breath with relief. So far so good, the king was taken in—but would Laurence notice anything different about him?

"I was walking by the wall, looking for ripe blackberries to eat, when I found something in the brambles. Something special."

"What did you find?" asked Maurice.

"A silver chalice, a very fine one, wrapped up in an old sack," continued Paud. "I had just opened it up and was looking at it when, out of nowhere, a horseman came by, knocked me to the ground and tried to snatch the chalice."

"Did you see who it was? What was the horse like?" the king interrupted.

"I don't like to say, Father," answered Paud, looking over at abbot Laurence.

"Tell them," said Brendan, blessing himself again as he spoke. In all his born days, he had never been part of a conspiracy or told a lie. Malachi had convinced him of the benefit of this plan but his conscience was still bothered by his part in it.

"It was the mason Maeldubh; I saw his red hair," Paud replied, looking at the circle of faces which surrounded him, at the worried frown of the elderly brother Brendan, the watchful suspicious look on Maurice Regan's face, the pursed angry expression of the abbot, above all, the black cloud that suddenly came over the king's face, blotting out the affection and good humour that had gone before.

"Do you mean a man who works here?" The king's voice was cold, controlled, mean.

Paud nodded. He felt his stomach heave and sweat break out on his forehead. Oh, for the safety of the Deerstone and an escape from all this, he thought. If only he could be certain they would save Luke, he would just scram, get himself out of this nightmare.

The faces began to blur, the tumult of voices grew louder and incomprehensible as if they had suddenly begun to speak in a language unknown to him. The sun seemed to be beating down directly on his head, making him feel faint and woozy. The world began to spin.

13

Majesty

It was the knocking that woke Paud up, or rather, a light tap-tapping, of wood on wood. It was there in the back of his consciousness but he was too exhausted to pay much attention to it or wonder what it was. The bed was warm and cosy and he was not inclined to get up just yet. Aunt Helen would be in soon enough to get him moving. He wriggled down further under the blanket, still in that drowsy state between sleep and wakefulness, when he began to realise that he was not in his own familiar bed. For a start, it didn't smell right. He opened an eye and pushed himself up on one elbow. He was lying on a low straw pallet in a long low-ceilinged room full of similar beds, like some kind of primitive boarding-school or hospital. The grey stone walls wept with condensation.

Paud realised with dismay that he was still in Glendalough and, what was worse, that he no longer had any idea how long he had been there. Was it possible that he had passed a night there? His mind raced back to the meeting with King Dermot—had he been caught out and put under arrest? His body certainly felt as if he had been beaten black and blue. Gingerly he pushed back the grey blanket which covered him and hauled himself to his feet. His head throbbed as he stood up, lances of pain shooting behind his eyes. He was taken aback to realise his head was bandaged. It was damp to the feel just behind his ear.

"Are you feeling better now? Is your head still bleeding?"

Paud swung around. On the floor on the opposite side of the room, a little girl was sitting, holding a sort of bat with a wooden ball dangling on a string. She looked at him and smiled, then pointed towards a bench near the door where two monks sat gently snoring and giggled.

Paud put his hand to his lips to warn her not to make a sound and tiptoed over to where she sat.

"Who are you?" he asked. "And where are we?"

"I'm your half-sister, Aoife. Dermot and Mór are my parents. And this is your sleeping-room, isn't it? Or have they put you in a different one?"

Paud relaxed a little—they still believed he was Luke.

"How long have I been here?"

Aoife shrugged. "About an hour. You fell in a faint and cut your head on a rock. The monks carried you here."

Paud sighed. This wasn't supposed to have happened. Now he didn't know what to do or what was happening.

"Aoife," he said, "will you help me to get out of here? Can you take a message to Malachi, the stone-mason, without them knowing?" He pointed towards the sleeping monks.

Aoife nodded. "What is the message?"

"Go to the priory, the new church they are building, and ask for Malachi. Don't talk to anyone else. You must trust only Malachi himself, do you understand?"

"I understand, but what am I to tell him?"

"Tell him I will meet him at the Deerstone when the monks go in to evening prayers."

"At the Deerstone? Where is that?" asked Aoife.

"He will know. Now hurry before those monks waken up. And, Aoife, come back afterwards. I need your help to get away from here."

Aoife nodded, picked up her wooden toy and tip-toed out of the room.

Paud gingerly eased himself back onto the bed which groaned and creaked beneath his weight. His two "minders," the snoring monks, shifted a little on their seats but slumbered on. It had begun to rain again: he could see the grey swirling squalls of rain at the window. A shiver ran down his body and, for the first time that day, he felt really frightened. How many hours had elapsed since he had sat on the Deerstone and wished himself back into this wild barbaric world? His head throbbed with pain and he felt a warm rush of nausea. Gingerly he touched the bandage behind his ear and probed the wet patch—was he badly hurt, he wondered, was it dangerous? God knows what rubbish they had put on it. And where was Malachi? Had he abandoned him? Paud's mind raced with all the possible outcomes—illness, capture, even death. No, he must stop thinking like this. The magic power of the stone was good and would keep him safe until Luke was free. They had together discovered a key to an ancient mystery: there had to be a reason for it.

One of the monks at the door stirred and rubbed his face with his hands. He looked over at the bed where Paud lay and smiled with satisfaction when he saw, or thought he saw, that the boy was still fast asleep.

"Brother Fidelmus, stir yourself, you have fallen asleep," he said, shaking the other monk by the shoulder. "The king and Abbot Laurence will be here shortly."

Indeed even as he spoke, Paud could hear the sound of approaching footsteps outside and a minute or two later, King Dermot was advancing upon him, with his full retinue of attendants and two or three monks following behind.

Paud sat up and made to get out of bed. He felt he would probably be expected to stand and bow before this magnificent, majestic "father," the very image of a king, but Dermot raised a hand to stop him.

"Luke, stay where you are. For an apprentice monk, you already look too battle-scarred. We want no more falls or injuries. Can you talk? Have you eaten?" He turned to the pair of sleepy monks who had been guarding Paud and shouted, "Have you brought my son food? Bring him soup, roast pig, curds, blackberries, bread, the best you have. He needs to be fattened up, ready for the journey."

"The journey, Father?" said Paud, weakly.

"Yes, Luke, you are to come back with me to Ferns. We shall leave tomorrow morning at first light." He turned to the abbot standing behind him. It was clear from the look on Laurence's face that this was the first he had heard of Luke's departure. "Abbot Laurence, it is better that Luke leaves with me. You can see that your kinsman Macdara and the rest of the O'Tooles have not accepted the hand of friendship which I offered them nine years ago when I married Mór O'Toole and appointed you here as abbot of Glendalough. They say they would rather be the rulers of these barren mountains than the kinsmen of the king of Leinster. So be it—but let me say this: I will secure the throne of all Ireland with or without their help. If it means that I have to make the very sods of Wicklow tremble beneath their feet so that their houses fall to the ground, their cattle flee in fear and their women cry out for mercy, then that is what I will do. Before the first snows lie on the Wicklow hills, the O'Tooles will rue the day they tried to block my way and to threaten my son."

"Come, come, good King Dermot," began Abbot Laurence, "this is not Christian talk." But Dermot ignored him and turned once again to Paud.

"Well, Luke, my youngest and most beloved son, will you come with me out of these rain-sodden hills and come to the castle at Ferns? I will make a soldier of you yet, and who knows, when we have all Ireland in our possession, we may even make a king of you."

It was no longer possible to delay, Paud now realised. He could not take the risk of being taken away from Glendalough, for it was only there that he had access to the Deerstone, his only means of escape back to his own time. If Malachi failed to find out where Luke was being held within the next few hours, Paud had no choice. He must get out. Yet he understood that the king's plan to take his son away was exactly what Luke would have wished, so he looked at the man who believed he was his father and said with a very serious expression, "Father, I shall be pleased to live with you at Ferns and to serve you with all my heart."

"Well said, Luke. You shall soon see my plans come to life, for I shall make of this land of ours a strong and a peaceful place. We shall impose order on all those tribes who do nothing but march against one another for sport, spilling the blood of their sons and brothers. I shall build ships to go to sea and trade with the Galls and the Norsemen and I shall build harbours along our coasts fit to shelter our sailing fleets and defend us from invasion. We shall have fine castles made of stone, the equal of which has never been seen even in England or France, and, moreover, there will be abbeys and monasteries, nunneries and great cathedrals in every diocese of Ireland, to give praise to our Lord God, Jesus Christ. I shall bring peace and scholarship and strength where now there is only division and weakness and uncertainty."

While the king was speaking, Aoife had come quietly back into Paud's sick-room, gave a low bow before her father and went to stand by the window. She gave a quick smile and nodded to Paud as she passed his bed.

"Father," she said, "there are riders coming very quickly down the mountain road where we came this morning."

Dermot and Laurence rushed to the window. Sure enough two horsemen were galloping down St Kevin's road. If they intended to stop at Glendalough they would be at the gates within minutes.

"Friend or foe, Laurence?" asked the king.

"Macdara's men, I should say. Strangers would not take such chances with their horses on these mountain roads. Those riders know the land."

"Brothers Fidelmus and Anselm, I leave to you the custody of my prince: lock up the doors and windows when we are gone and let no-one pass in or out until I myself come to relieve you." The king's voice was hard and cold. He had not forgotten the carelessness of Brother Brendan earlier that morning.

"Go with God and be sure—Luke will come to no harm while he is in our care," replied Fidelmus, making the sign of the cross, whereupon King Dermot led his men out of the dormitory without another word.

The abbot Laurence paused until they heard the outer door slam with a loud thud, then turned to look at Paud with a puzzled expression. "There is something strange about you today, my young Luke, and Brother Brendan is as jumpy as the salmon in the Glendasan river. Think hard before you get up to any trickery— remember the Lord above sees everything—but I also have eyes in the back of my head."

His eyes remained fixed for a moment on Paud's, who felt himself colouring with embarrassment but was unable to break the abbot's spell on him by lowering his face. "The king may well be right to take you away from here," continued Laurence. "Life here is not suitable for one so young—you will be glad to leave us."

Before Paud could think of a reply, there came a great shouting and laughing from the stable yard nearby.

"Now what can that be, Brother Fidelmus?" the abbot asked and he hurriedly left Paud with his two minders (and Aoife, whom everybody seemed to have forgotten) to see who was now disturbing the peace of the city.

14

Macdara's Messengers

The rain which had persisted since early morning had finally stopped. The sun shone brightly and a fresh warm breeze gently stirred the surface of the two lakes. Malachi walked briskly up through the trees, avoiding the road the horsemen had taken earlier: he had no wish to be seen by anyone leaving or entering Glendalough. He reckoned that four hours had passed since Luke's seizure by Maeldubh—four hours too many, four hours in the hands of a dangerous and unstable man who might not flinch at inflicting great hurt on the boy. The bitterness between King Dermot and the old O'Toole dynasty went deep: yet Dermot had become a good king and a just man; of the four provinces of Ireland, Leinster was the most secure, the least scarred by battle. His people were loyal to him—all but this chieftain, Macdara.

What neither Malachi nor Macdara knew was how much the king loved his own son, Luke. Macdara *thought* he knew; that was why he was prepared to seize the boy and hold him as a hostage until the king responded to his demands. Malachi had not wanted the king to know that Luke had been kidnapped for the simple reason that Dermot might let Luke languish in captivity. The king was not the type of man who would give in to threats—and ambitious men could be ruthless, even in dealings with their own family. Had not the king already taken Luke away from his own mother and sent him to be fostered with the monks so that the O'Tooles might accept Dermot as their king? Had he not married Mór O'Toole for the same reason? But if they refused to accept his rule, Macdara O'Toole should know that the king Dermot would burn his enemies out of the Wicklow woods and would not rest until he had them all in fetters rather than give up an inch of territory. And if it came to battle, Luke would surely lose his life.

Malachi would see to it that he did not. He was intent on reaching Macdara's mountain fort in the forest and finding out where Luke was being held. Meanwhile Paud would act the part of Luke, making nonsense of the ransom demanded by the messengers Macdara had sent to Glendalough.

Malachi had earlier seen the men, the brothers Carbery and Thomas, when they arrived breathless at the sanctuary stone at the gateway into the monastery, demanding safe passage to speak to "Abbot Laurence and Dermot of Ferns." Anselm, the master of the guest-house, who had gone to the gate when he had seen the horsemen come down the valley, bade them wait outside while he went to look for the abbot and added that he knew no-one of the name of Dermot of Ferns unless they meant Dermot Mac Murrough, king of all of the province of Leinster.

He would have let them cool their heels for half an hour or more for he had not liked their rough manners but the king himself, hearing the noise of the horses, had come out into the yard with Maurice Regan and the abbot.

"Whoever asks for sanctuary must be granted it," agreed Laurence at once. "But on holy ground, no-one may carry arms. Leave your knives and swords there on the ground and we shall welcome you as our guests."

Carbery and Thomas, after some argument among themselves, removed their knives from their leather belts and threw them some feet away where Anselm picked them up and carried them off for safe-keeping. The great wooden gate was hauled open and the two young messengers walked through the arch into Glendalough.

The yard was full by this time, many of the monks and labourers having left their work to come and see what the commotion was. They relished any disturbance of their usual quiet and uneventful lives and stood around curiously in groups. King Dermot stood in the centre of the courtyard, his chest pushed out, his thumbs tucked behind the gold buckle of his belt. Behind him stood Maurice Regan, his restless eyes darting about as he summed up the appearance of the two new arrivals and the danger his master might be in. The king's captain-at-arms and seven of his men had spread out unnoticed to encircle the crowd. Two stable-hands walked forward to lead away the messengers' sweating horses. Abbot Laurence asked the two men to kneel on the ground in front of him.

"Why do you seek the sanctuary of the Church?" he asked.

"I am Carbery, this is my brother, both of us messengers of Macdara, our lord and kinsman. We ask only for safe passage so that we can give our message and leave in peace," said Carbery, his voice steady.

"Who is your message to?"

"For Dermot of Ferns and Laurence O'Toole," replied Carbery as a shocked whisper ran around the onlookers. It was the height of rudeness not to use the title of the king. Dermot's right hand slid towards the short sword which hung in a silver scabbard from his belt. His soldiers moved a step or two nearer.

"I am Laurence O'Toole, abbot of Glendalough. I do not know the other man you seek, unless you mean Dermot, king of Leinster."

"I have it on good authority from one who works here that Dermot of Ferns arrived here before noon this morning. Let us not play games. I have news for him concerning his son Lugaid, or Luke as he is also known."

Malachi's attention at this moment had been distracted by the sight of Brother Brendan slipping quietly out of the yard and taking the path towards the scriptorium. When he looked again, the king had moved forward with two of his men and was standing over Carbery and his companion.

"This is holy ground," he was saying, "and the abbot has granted you sanctuary so I will obey the law of the church. I am Dermot, native of Ferns as you say, but I am also your king and will have the honour shown to me that is due to a king."

"We pay tribute to Macdara who is lord of these lands. We can only accept as our king and overlord whoever Macdara honours—and we know of no King Dermot." Thomas, who had been silent until now, spoke softly, laying a hand on Carbery's arm. "But we bring you a message which you will do well to hear."

Maurice Regan now walked forward and all began to speak in low urgent voices. Malachi strained to listen but could make out nothing more until King Dermot threw his head back and with a great roar of laughter shouted, "But Macdara is a fool! My son is safe and well within these walls!"

"Then you surely have not seen him these past hours." Carbery responded as quick as a flash.

"Why, we left him only moments ago when we heard your horses approaching at a gallop," retorted Dermot.

Carbery shot a look towards Thomas. What trickery was this? Had they not seen the boy themselves less than two hours ago on the back of Maeldubh's horse at Macdara's fort? Maurice Regan saw the look exchanged between the messengers and saw the flicker of doubt in their eyes.

"As a loyal servant of King Dermot, and an obedient servant of the church which has granted you sanctuary, I shall not order the men here to throw you in irons," said Maurice coldly. "But listen well! A traitorous mason did indeed make an assault on the prince some hours ago, but he failed to seize him or to injure him. If Maeldubh says otherwise, he is a liar! If Maeldubh says he has the boy, the boy is an impostor and is plotting with the mason to deceive your lord Macdara." He stopped a moment to let the full meaning of what he was saying sink in. The words liar, impostor, plot, deceive, seeped into the air of the yard like the smell of rotting meat. No-one dared move.

"Come, let us show you the king's son, safe in our care," the abbot's voice broke the silence, "so you can understand how Maeldubh is deceiving you and your chief. Then, in good faith, we will be happy to offer you meat and drink for your journey before you quit our city. But you will not return here for you bring shame on the good name of the O'Toole tribe."

As the king's group moved away towards the monks' sleeping quarters where Paud was under guard, Malachi had gone in search of Brother Brendan whom he found nervously pacing up and down his work-room.

"Brendan, take courage," he said as soon as he entered, embracing his old friend. "Do as you have promised me and I will return Luke to Glendalough and to his father without fail. When Carbery and Thomas are taken off to eat, have Fidelmus prepare a strong sleeping draught and add it to the wine Anselm brings them—it is important that they do not return to Macdara's fort before I have done my work. Now go and see the stranger from the Deerstone—he is a brave boy but he needs our help too."

"Stop! Put your hands on your head and say what business you have here." Malachi was jolted out of his day-dreaming by the rough voice. He cautiously brought his hands up to his head and turned slightly to his left to see who had spoken. In the shadow of the trees he caught a glimpse of a familiar burly figure.

"Don't move. What is your business here?" Malachi could hear the snap of a twig underfoot as the man drew nearer.

"You know me well, Maeldubh, as well as I know your voice for I am your master Malachi, the stone-mason from Glendalough. I am going to speak to Macdara O'Toole."

"Who has sent you?" Maeldubh demanded angrily.

"I will speak to none but Macdara himself," replied Malachi. Another twig cracked, close by, the sound coming from barely six feet behind his back.

"Then you will speak to no-one!" came the reply. At the same moment Malachi saw the flash of a blade glint in the dappled sunlight of the forest but he was ready for the assault. He turned and sprang upon his attacker. The knife struck his right shoulder but fell away to the ground as Malachi's powerful left fist caught Maeldubh's chin. Maeldubh staggered back as he lost his balance but recovered quickly from the suddenness of Malachi's counter-attack and lunged again. The two men crashed to the ground, rolling over and over again as each struggled to win control, kicking and lashing out with their fists. Both were tall, muscular men, fit from the rigours of working with stone: neither would easily outdo the other. Maeldubh was the first to see where the knife had fallen. He stretched out an arm, his fingers scrabbling desperately among the leaves to get a grip.

Malachi, pinned to the earth under Maeldubh's weight, fought to stop him, vainly trying to pull him in the opposite direction away from the knife.

"You—took—the—wrong—boy," gasped Malachi. He could feel Maeldubh's sharp intake of breath before he made one final lunge for the knife. Malachi leapt to his feet, only seconds ahead of his attacker, and ran for the higher open ground above the trees. As they broke cover, two large hounds, barking furiously, came rushing towards them and might have thrown themselves at Malachi's neck to tear him limb from limb had they not reached the end of the ropes which tethered them to a post.

Maeldubh stopped running, shouted at the dogs to stop their barking, and gestured at Malachi to walk on—his heels only inches from the snapping teeth of the hounds, and at his back the mason's menacing knife. They had arrived at the O'Tooles' mountain stronghold.

Macdara's house was built of stone, its low walls built under the shelter of the hill-side, so that it was almost concealed from view between the woods and the mountain towering above. There was one great arched door leading into a filthy inner yard where the pigs and hens were cooped, and which smelled of damp straw and animal manure. Maeldubh marched Malachi through this, ignoring the stares of the men who came out to see who the stranger was. From the yard another door led into a small hall that also served as Macdara's main living-room. A fire was burning in the huge hearth, the damp logs spitting and sputtering as the

flames dried them out. Of Macdara himself there was no sign.

Down the centre of the hall was a long oak trestle table with a bench on each side and near the hearth was a low stool with a harp sitting next to it. Maeldubh snorted with annoyance when no-one answered his summonses and roughly pushed Malachi towards another door. This brought them into a dark, smoky kitchen, its only ventilation a hole in the roof—and that clearly didn't work well. As Malachi's eyes grew used to the gloom, he made out the figure of a manservant basting a piece of meat at the fire. The floor of beaten earth had been stirred up into a quagmire of mud because of the heavy rains earlier. Maeldubh crossed the room, kicking out at the hens which wandered freely in and out pecking at fallen bits of food, and angrily ordered the servant to leave them. He stopped in front of what looked like a heap of rags lying in the corner and shook it roughly. The rags stirred and sat up.

"Malachi!" exclaimed Luke, rubbing his eyes, "is it really you? I've just been dreaming—I'm sure Paud is at the Deerstone."

It was too late. Maeldubh stepped forward and grabbed Luke roughly by the shoulder. "What do you say about the Deerstone? Who did you say was there?"

15
Ancient Powers

Paud stopped running as he came within sight of the bridge and, just beyond it, the Deerstone. The stones were bathed in a pool of golden sunlight, drawing him towards them as if by a sort of magnetic force: there lay safety. The voice in his head was becoming clearer. It was as if he had finely tuned a radio which before was just picking up crackly voices and scratchy bits of music. He could hear Luke's voice now, so clearly that at first he thought that Luke must have escaped from his captors and was hiding somewhere nearby, but there was no-one to be seen down by the river except one solitary monk collecting rushes.

Paud walked past him without a word and the monk paid no heed to him. Only a few more steps now and he would be sitting on the Deerstone. Luke's voice was becoming urgent: Paud must sit on the stone and make the wish. But what wish? Surely he couldn't be telling him to leave Glendalough and return to his own time. No, Paud would not go, would not run away before

Luke was safely back. If only Malachi had come to him as he promised Aoife he would—then Malachi could help him guess what Luke wanted him to do.

His fingers pressed into the hollows where Cronan the master mason had all those centuries before left his prints. "Help me to hear what Luke is saying," he sighed.

A great stillness came over him; he felt neither awake nor asleep, but in some place between the real world and the world of dreams. The little monastic city appeared to be arrested in time, immobilised, the tower and cathedral fading in and out of focus, then captured for one fleeting second as if by an unseen camera in a blinding flash of light.

"Wish for me to come to you. Paud, wish for me to come to you." Luke's voice came to him, clear as a bell but anxious, rising in desperation.

Paud grasped the rock and wished with all his might. Every cell of his body, every muscle, every drop of blood coursing through his veins ached with the effort of concentration. Could he unlock the power of the Deerstone to do such a thing? This was why he had been brought to this wild barbaric city. He alone could release Luke from wherever he was being held through the mysterious and ancient power of the stone. It had already moved him through the dimension of time— now he would invoke the spirit of the stones, endowed with the power to protect children, to move Luke through space, physically to carry him to the sanctuary of the Deerstone. "Please, please, let Luke come here to me now."

A great wave of energy seemed to surge through his body, emanating from the stone beneath his fingers. The shadowy, insubstantial figure of Luke began to take shape in front of Paud's incredulous eyes. He could just make out his "twin's" pale face, his long fringe, the ankle-length tunic before the figure faded and disappeared from view. Paud gripped the stone and wished again but the figure of Luke did not reappear. The power which he had tapped from deep within the Deerstone had ebbed away. What had he done? Had he destroyed the power of the stone by asking too much of it? Had he not only lost Luke now but also all chance of getting out himself? His stomach heaved and sweat broke out on his forehead as the panic engulfed him.

Once more he traced the hollow fingerprints of the Deerstone and wished, "Wherever Luke may be, let him hear this wish and make him come to me."

At that moment Paud heard a great roar from a long way off which sent shivers down his spine. He felt dizzy, afraid that he might lose consciousness again as he had done earlier. He could hear Luke calling to him but there was a great clamour of other voices too, confusing him, breaking his will to save Luke.

The walls of the city seemed to melt away; he could no longer see the round tower or the thatched roofs of the churches, nor could he hear the swishing of the rushes as the monk cut them from the river bank and tied them into bunches. Directly ahead of him appeared a dull red glow. The voices seemed to be coming from there, one encouraging, the other commanding him to come forward. Paud could not say how or when he had left the Deerstone but now found himself walking through an arched wooden door into a large hall. The red light which he had followed was the smouldering remains of a log fire in a large stone hearth. At either end of a long oak table sat the two masons Malachi and Maeldubh.

"Come forward, boy," ordered Maeldubh.

Paud advanced a few steps. He was beyond fear now, beyond panic or despair, transported into a world whose rules he did not know. As soon as he had seen Malachi and Maeldubh together, he knew his earlier fears had been right—the powers that the masons drew from the stones were not always benevolent. They could be tapped for good or evil purposes—and he had been pitted against Maeldubh in the battle for supremacy.

Maeldubh, sitting at the head of the table nearest the fire, no longer seemed the rain-soaked ill-tempered mason that Paud had seen beating the donkey that morning. Now he seemed a more deadly and dangerous opponent, radiating strength. His unkempt shoulder-length red hair gleamed like an exotic copper head-dress; his wide green eyes flashed with contempt. Could Paud stand up to him?

"Do not be afraid," said Malachi, as if reading Paud's thoughts. Malachi too looked different, older and broader, bigger in every respect, but in contrast to the menace given off by Maeldubh, Malachi radiated serenity and friendship.

"What do you want?" asked Paud.

"I am giving you the chance to save your skin, to get

out of here whence you came, before I undo the power of the Deerstone for ever." Maeldubh leant across the table and fixed Paud with his wild staring eyes.

"No, be strong, Paud, do not listen to him," interrupted Malachi. "You must save Luke. Only by saving Luke first can you save yourself. If you turn your back on him, there is no knowing if the power of the Deerstone which brought you here will still be strong enough to take you back to your own time and your own people."

"Where is Luke now?" Paud's voice came out as a croak.

"He is in what we call the Shadow World, neither here nor in the other world. You summoned him to join you but your will failed before he could reach you," Malachi answered sombrely. Maeldubh gave a snort of derision.

"My will did not fail," protested Paud. "I wanted him to come but something was fighting against me, pulling Luke away from me. Malachi, can we get him back?"

"Only you can save him now but you will have to pit your will against Maeldubh. Good must triumph, Paud; your responsibility is great. If you do not succeed, the forces of evil will be unleashed on the whole land. Those, like Dermot and Laurence, who stand for change and progress will be driven out and instead the old exhausted ways will prevail, dragging our province back into the darkest ages." He paused a moment and smiled sympathetically at Paud's stricken face. "But, have courage, I will fight for you against Maeldubh and the evil uses to which he puts his stone-mason's powers. As he creates doubt, I shall give you certainty. As he plants despair, I shall bring you hope."

"What must I do, then?" said Paud.

"You must decide that for yourself." Malachi stood up and walked to Paud's right side. Maeldubh, whose eyes had never left Paud for one second, leered at him.

Paud's eyes closed. He could still see the dull red glow of the embers in the fireplace in front of him but, at the same time, he had the sensation of being carried off by a great whooshing wind high above and out of reach of both the stone-masons.

He was suspended in space above Glendalough with a bird's eye view of everything below him. But it was no longer the Glendalough of Luke that lay beneath him but the Glendalough in ruins, of his own time. The little stone churches stood forlorn and roofless, the stone wall which Paud knew had surrounded the little city had all but disappeared and where it still existed was only a few feet in height; the brown-robed monk who had been tying up the bundles of rushes down by the river was gone; he could see neither cattle grazing nor hens scratching among the stones. The city lay wounded and abandoned, an air of melancholy hanging over it and over the whole valley. In the modern car park near the visitors' centre there was just one large coach, the one Paud had travelled in that morning, where he could just make out the faces of the other children at the windows. A small group of adults were standing outside the coach, in earnest conversation. He recognised his teacher, Mr Burke, and Dave, the driver.

"Go, Paud, go," whispered a low voice, "this is where you belong. Make your wish and get back to your own people, your own time. Listen how they are worrying about you."

"He's not a bad lad," Mr Burke was saying to Dave. "He wouldn't just have run off again—no, I'm sure he must be in some sort of trouble. We'll have to call the police and get up a proper search party. What his parents will say, I dread to think."

With a shock, Paud remembered his parents. He had almost forgotten the other life he belonged to. Suddenly he was repelled by the filth, the stench, the dirty, foul-smelling, primitive, cruel world he had found himself in, and longed to be free of it. He would go back and leave them to their own devices—he was no more a part of their world than they were a part of his. The image of the coach grew faint. Paud felt himself drifting towards the Deerstone.

"Paud, Paud, can you hear me?" Luke's face, pale and ghost-like, materialised beside him. "Don't leave me here in the Shadow World. If you go away, I will never be able to go back to my father or even to the monks in Glendalough."

Paud stretched out a hand to Luke but touched nothing. He no longer knew where he was or what was real or imagined. He was so exhausted, so confused, he just wanted to be able to put an end to the whole nightmare. Who was he to trust? Could Maeldubh really undo the power of the Deerstone? And if he fought to rescue Luke first, would he still be able to save himself afterwards or would the stone have lost its power? Or was Malachi right—unless he saved Luke and used the power of the Deerstone for good, he would not be able to unlock its power to travel back to modern Ireland. How was he to know if he could have more than one wish?

"Paud, wish me back to life. The Deerstone will not fail us," Luke's disembodied voice whispered at him.

In the car park there was a police car reversing into place beside the coach, and figures running. Their voices, calling his name, pierced the deathly stillness of the valley. With one wish Paud knew he could be back there, travelling comfortably back to his home in Dublin where his parents would soon be arriving from their trip to France. He had been unfair about them— being sent to a summer camp wasn't like banishment, wasn't the worst thing in the world to happen to you.

Poor Luke. He too had been left behind by his father. But King Dermot planned to take him home—and Luke didn't know that! Luke didn't even know that his father was there in Glendalough. He had been kidnapped before he got back down to the city. Paud felt a great rush of joy for his twin-friend—yes, he would wish him out of Maeldubh's power and back to Glendalough— Malachi was the one to trust. Maeldubh had to be wrong. His fingers slipped over to his left—yes, he had drifted back to the Deerstone. Perhaps he had never left. As he tightened his grasp on the rock and closed his eyes, a strong current of energy flowed through his body. This was it. He formed his words carefully:

"The Deerstone saved the lives of two boys once before. Let it do so again."

When he opened his eyes again, a monk carrying a long bundle of rushes was running towards him. Paud jumped off the Deerstone in alarm, thinking he was going to be beaten but the monk suddenly threw himself onto the ground before his feet. "God have mercy upon me. I am just a poor ignorant man. Tell me the meaning of this vision."

Paud felt a tug at his sleeve and turned around. There stood Luke at his side.

16

As Alike As Two Sparrows

After that Paud and Luke seemed to know instinctively what they had to do. They walked side by side across the damp wicker bridge which creaked beneath their steps, and still without speaking, turned to the bramble bushes under which the chalice of Murchad, still wrapped in its jute sacking, lay hidden. Luke picked it up and passed it to Paud.

"You found it, you must return it. Put down your hood: there is no need for disguise any more. We shall go into the city as brothers."

The monk who had watched Paud sitting on the Deerstone and who had seen Luke materialise out of the blue was excitedly calling several of the other monks and labourers from the fields and this small group followed the boys across the stream. As they pushed their hoods off their faces, revealing as it seemed not one Luke, but two, many of the monks stopped in their tracks and broke out in a chorus of exclamations.

Paud and Luke ignored them.

"Call Brother Brendan," someone cried.

"Run and fetch the abbot," cried another.

"The king, the king," urged someone else.

Luke turned to Paud in surprise. "The king? Do they mean my father?"

"Yes," smiled Paud. "He was the visitor you saw coming down the mountains this morning. He is going to take you home with him. He doesn't know that you were taken hostage by Maeldubh—only Brother Brendan and Malachi know what happened. I pretended to be you. It's a long story, Luke, but first, let us tell the news that you are safe. Come on."

By now more and more curious monks and labourers had joined the procession behind the "twins" while others ran ahead, calling out for Abbot Laurence and Brother Brendan to come quickly, so that there was already quite a commotion as they arrived at the door of the guest-room. Before they could even knock, the heavy oak door was pulled open and Brother Brendan appeared.

"What is all this noise? Don't you know the king is resting?" All at once his mouth flew open as he saw the boys.

"Luke?" he asked. "Or are you the other one? How did you leave Anselm and Fidelmus? And if you are truly Luke, how do you come to be here?"

"It was a miracle! I saw it with my own eyes. The second Luke appeared out of the sky, down by the stream. I was cutting rushes..." A monk pushed forward to the front of the group. "I saw it happen. He made his own double. Tell us, Brendan, what can it mean? Is he flesh or spirit? Is it the end of our world. What is to become of us in these strange times?"

"That is enough, Brother Colman, hold your tongue a minute, let the boys come forward."

He stretched out an arm and pulled the boys into the guest-house, banging the door behind them with a resounding thud.

Once inside, Brendan ushered them towards the wooden bench beside the hearth and bade them sit down where he could see them in the light of the fire.

One by one, he looked at them, putting his hand under their chins and lifting up their faces to examine them the better.

"No, you are as alike as two sparrows. I cannot say which of you is Luke."

"I am Luke, Brother Brendan. And this, as I think you know, is my friend Paud, who has saved me from Maeldubh who took me hostage to insult my father."

"I am so happy to see you well and in safe hands, Luke—I have never been so worried—but before you tell me how you got away, I must know how Paud comes to be with you. Surely," Brendan continued, looking at Paud and wringing his hands, "my brother monks Anselm and Fidelmus did not let you go freely out of their sight?"

"It was easy," admitted Paud. "Everyone had forgotten about Aoife. That's your sister," he added to Luke. "She was great. When the two messengers came from Macdara, or Maeldubh, whoever sent them..."

"You mean, Carbery and his brother, who came asking for your ransom, I mean, Luke's ransom," said

Brendan, casting a nervous glance at the door which led upstairs to the king's quarters.

"Yes, well, when they came in to be shown that 'Luke' had not been captured at all, there was a great argument, with a lot of shouting and explaining. The king and all the king's men and you and the abbot and the monks who were guarding me and Macdara's men and more monks beside that. It was easy in all the confusion to get out of the bed and Aoife slipped into it in my place. I suppose she pretended to fall fast asleep—she is probably there still, with Anselm and Fidelmus watching over her!"

"But where did you go?" Brendan asked.

"Straight to the Deerstone. I thought Malachi would be waiting for me there."

"But," interrupted Luke, "Malachi was in the house where Maeldubh had taken me."

Brendan put up a hand to stop him. "I can see this is a long tale and, since each of us has his part to tell, let me call the abbot and the king and all who need to hear it and the story can be told from the beginning. But I fear we have not come to the end of it yet."

At length the questions ceased and there was a long silence during which there was nothing to be heard but the gentle collapse of powdery logs in the hearth and the lowing of the cows in the meadow by the lake. Each man present wondered at the strange story he had just heard—of Luke's kidnap by Maeldubh and of his rescue by a boy from another age who had the power to move through time and space, a power he said that came from the Deerstone—and each time he thought it must be all invention, he looked up and saw the faces of the two boys, as like as two hazelnuts.

Maurice Regan, sitting by the king's right hand, was the first to speak.

"What has become of Malachi?"

This was a question that had been bothering Paud too.

Luke had told them how he had seen Malachi at the house in the woods where he had been held captive and how at first Malachi had pretended not to recognise him. Malachi had laughed at Maeldubh, saying he had made the O'Toole name a laughing stock—even Carbery and his brother Thomas would be ashamed to return from the monastery, after having been mocked as fools for asking for a ransom for Luke when Luke was perfectly safe back in Glendalough. They had seen him with their own eyes.

Maeldubh was confused long enough for the seed of doubt that Malachi had planted to grow larger. "Who then is this?" he had asked, pointing at Luke.

"Nothing but spirit," replied Malachi, "a changeling called out of the dark ages by your unconscious, such is your spite for Dermot and Laurence. I dare say I can send him away again! By the ancient powers of the stones which we both possess, I challenge you to stop me."

It was then that Luke had begun to hear Paud's voice, calling to him from the Deerstone, and struggled to understand what he was saying. The rope which tied him to the stone in the corner of the kitchen no longer chafed at his ankle—yet he was still tied to it. It was as if he was drifting above his body, above the world. Just as Paud had described it, Luke could see the two masons who had taken up position at either end of the the table in the long hall, pitting their ancient stone-carver's powers against one another, Malachi inspiring Paud to believe in the energy of the stone and pull Luke to safety. Luke could see Paud's white face becoming clearer, so solid he was reaching out to take hold of him when all at once, Maeldubh seemed to realise how he was being tricked and let out a great roar of anger, the same roar that Paud had heard as he sat on the Deerstone.

"There *are* two of them," Maeldubh had shouted, his face contorted with rage. "I conjured up no spirit! They are the twins of the Deerstone!"

Maurice Regan had heard the story through in silence but now he spoke the question that had begun to nag at Paud. "And what will have become of Malachi?" he asked.

"How can the boys tell?" answered the abbot. "This story, I make no secret of it, troubles me greatly. It is always dangerous to call up those powers they say reside in the ancient stones and it were better if no-one had done so. We must have faith that Malachi will return when he can."

"Tell me again, Abbot Laurence, about this handsome chalice they have found." King Dermot lifted the chalice from the table in front of him and ran his fingers around the filigree gold border of the stem.

"As Brother Brendan has said, it was a gift to the cathedral in the will of King Murchad, the last O'Toole to be the king of Leinster, may he rest in peace—he is buried here at Reefert in the royal graveyard. The chalice was made to his father's own design—or so the story goes, probably about one hundred years ago—and was carried into battle by the O'Tooles as a portent of good luck. A superstition, not to be counted upon."

"Be that as it may, Abbot Laurence, the O'Toole chiefs, for I will not call them kings, believe it to be theirs and were prepared to steal it back." Maurice Regan had got no further when the bell of the round tower began to ring out urgently—the terrible sequence of short peals that spelt danger. The king and Regan turned to one another in alarm as the abbot rushed to the door. There was no doubt in their minds— Glendalough was once again under attack.

17

Into Battle

It was the king's captain, Donnell Macdermott, on watch at the top of the round tower, who had sounded the alarm. He had seen the approach of Macdara and his men as they rode down into the valley from the west. There was no mistaking their mission—they were heavily slung about with swords and axes, slings and javelins and one of the party bore aloft a large flaming torch—as they put their horses to the gallop on the flat approach to the city. There were at least twenty of them, the captain guessed, while he had only seven of the king's soldiers under his command in the advance party that had arrived that morning—and they had not only the king and his children to protect but the whole unarmed community of monks. It was going to be an unequal struggle.

He was hauling open the door—which was more than twelve feet off the ground—and preparing to throw down the rope ladder just as the king arrived at the tower.

"To horse, captain, and leave the monks to guard the tower and its treasures. It seems Macdara is spoiling for a fight."

Even as the king spoke, the soldiers were leading out their horses from the stables and saddling them up. The abbot, surrounded on all sides by his brother monks, was issuing commands. This one was to close up the main gates, that one to climb up into the tower and keep watch; others were to take the older monks and children and make their way as speedily as they could down the new Green Road through the woods to the safety of the new priory.

"And stay there until the bells ring out again to let you know it is safe to return. Go with God," shouted Laurence as Fidelmus led his little group away towards the trees.

Yet others started to round up the cattle and pigs—so many animals had been robbed or killed in recent raids that the monks could ill afford more losses.

Even as the thunder of galloping hooves grew louder and the war-cries of Macdara and his men ever closer, the community of Glendalough prepared for battle with calmness and resolution.

Paud and Luke did not wait to be told to join the group heading for the new priory but looked at one another and nodded.

"Come on, Luke, follow me."

*

Crouching in the shelter of the boundary wall, Paud pulled off his borrowed tunic and hastily pulled on his jeans and sweatshirt and tied up the laces of his trainers. His heart was pounding with fear—and excitement too. Things were happening so fast but he knew he had to keep a cool head and be ready for a quick getaway if the worst came to the worst. As he buckled on his watch-strap, he noticed it said 19:36. In the summer in Dublin it usually got dark very late, about ten o'clock, but light was already beginning to fade. Every instinct told Paud he must be gone soon, must not take the risk of spending a night away from his own time.

Luke was jumpy too. "Hurry, Paud, we're not safe here any longer."

As he spoke, a great clamour could be heard at the main gateway. The boys crept forward, keeping close together in the shadow of the church buildings—as they drew nearer, they could make out two figures high up on top of the gate tower locked in hand to hand struggle. The city had already been breached—Macdara's men had entered Glendalough. Another great roar rent the air as the heavy wooden gates gave way under fierce battering and the mounted figure of Macdara O'Toole rode in under the arch. He made an awesome spectacle, mounted on a dark black horse which reared up on its hind legs. Macdara himself was entirely dressed in black and had a jet-black barbarous beard which reached down to his chest. Above his head he brandished a fearsome-looking battleaxe. Beside Macdara came another figure that both Paud and Luke now knew well: the chieftain's kinsman but their enemy, the hateful stone-mason Maeldubh. Behind them came Macdara's warriors, pouring in through the gateway and yelling and screaming as if their lungs would burst.

"What should we do?" cried Luke.

"Quick, to the Deerstone. Run," shouted Paud, intent now on escape at any price, but they were stopped in their tracks as a volley of flaming fireballs flew over their heads, landing among the thatched houses of the monks. Within moments the roofs had gone up in flames.

"Turn to the guest-house," cried Luke. "We can shelter in there."

As they ran, they saw the most extraordinary sight emerge from behind the trees by the river—a group of monks on horseback charged forward, their leader a huge hooded man carrying a long javelin.

"Look, Paud, they are not monks—that is my father and those are his soldiers."

And indeed it looked as if Luke was right. They saw Macdara turn—Paud noticed they all rode without saddles—and whip his horse into a gallop. The two groups bore down on each other, javelins and daggers at the ready.

The boys could hear the crash of iron on iron and the frantic whinnies of the horses as they reached the guest-house and pulled back the heavy wooden bars on the door to barricade themselves in.

"We can see what happens from the window upstairs," said Luke, running towards the stairs.

Outnumbered as they were, the kings' men fought hard and furiously, being more skilled in the practice of war than the wild Wicklow men—and better armed too. Their sudden appearance dressed as monks had unsettled some of Macdara's men who at first seemed reluctant to join in the attack on the "holy men." They hung back at the rear or rode around in a frenzy, shouting their battle-cries and putting up a strange and frightening show of ferocity. King Dermot launched himself upon Macdara, his javelin thrust out ahead of him, but just as he was within striking distance, Maeldubh came at him in a gallop from the side and caught the flank of the king's horse with his battleaxe. The boys watched, horror-stricken, as the horse rose up on its hind legs in an agony of pain.

At the same moment, Paud saw Maeldubh put his hand to the back of his head before toppling in slow motion to the ground.

"What happened him?" Paud asked.

"Someone threw something which hit him on the head." Luke pointed down by the trees. "It must be the masons, look over there. They must have come up to to help defend the city. I have heard they hurl flat stones at their enemies in battle but I have never seen such a thing before. But Paud, can you see my father? His horse threw him when it was hurt. Is he on the ground?"

The boys craned to see where the king had fallen but the narrow window gave them a very restricted view of the battle and the fading light made it hard to distinguish the king and his men in their dark monks' habits. In any case, the situation changed so quickly as the horsemen launched attack and counter-attack. The city was now enveloped in a thick pall of smoke billowing from the blazing thatches of the dwellings.

"I must know if he has come to harm," said Luke. "I'm going out there. Will you come?"

Paud nodded solemnly and followed Luke down the stairs. They pulled back the iron bolts of the door and walked out into the fray.

The king's massive horse, Brandub, lay dead at the foot of the round tower, the grass beneath him stained red from the blood which still trickled from the ugly gash in his haunch. The king was nowhere to be seen but the main area of battle had moved away from the monastery buildings and was now closer to the river.

"He can't have been hurt by the fall," said Paud. "He must have got away."

"Perhaps he took another horse from someone else who had been hit. Maybe he even seized Maeldubh's horse when Maeldubh was knocked off by the flying stone." Luke nervously looked around, hoping the mason was not suddenly going to appear for he was sickened by the sights of the fighting and had no stomach for another confrontation.

Paud knew how he was feeling. "Yes, you're right. Maeldubh cannot have been too badly hurt either or we'd see him lying around here somewhere." If only Malachi had come back, he was thinking. What can have happened to him after Luke got away?

"Luke," said Paud, "we have to get to the Deerstone. It is the only way to stop all this."

"But Paud, we can't go down there—listen, can't you hear that that's where the noise of the fighting is coming from, down there by the river."

"Don't you see, we have no choice. Malachi needs us to go there to save him. We have to believe in the protection of the stone. It saved you. Now it can bring all this fighting to an end and send Macdara and his men packing for good."

Paud felt he had come to a point of no return. If there was any explanation for his travelling through time to this ancient city and for him to have been chosen, not anybody else, then it must be because there was something that he had to do there. Skulking around behind stone walls and keeping out of sight was not helping anyone—he and Luke must boldly walk out into the battle—either the spirit of the Deerstone would keep them safe or it would not.

"Was that chalice still on the table where King Dermot left it?"

"I think so," said Luke.

"Well, let's go and take it and then go to the Deerstone. We need all the protection we can get."

Hugging the silver chalice closely against his chest, Paud walked briskly towards the wicker bridge which would lead him directly to the safety of the Deerstone. Behind him came Luke, running a little to keep up, both of them moving fearlessly through the battle which still raged around them and keeping their eyes fixed at all times on the stones which were their talisman. The air was thick with acrid smoke and the sweaty smell of horses. Dusk was drawing in faster, sealing the valley in a dark embrace.

The twins walked on, drawn towards the stones which radiated that magnetic pull which had earlier attracted them and ignoring the wild screams all around them as the fighters lunged at one another, the sickening crash of blade on blade and the stone missiles which hurtled through the air from the trees beyond the still black surface of the lake. But if they ignored the gory scenes around him, the same could not be said of some of Macdara's men, who drew back and stood transfixed by fright, imagining they were seeing a vision as the twins passed by—Paud dressed in his outlandish garb and bearing the silver chalice of Murchad, with his double, Luke, close on his heels.

A silence fell upon the valley and the eyes of all the warriors followed the boys as they crossed the bridge and stood before the Deerstone. Paud raised the chalice above his head and jumped up onto the hollow bowl-shaped stone which had so long ago been used to hold the milk for the stone-mason's baby infants. Luke stood on his left on the large stone which bore the finger-marks of Cronan when he had invested the stones with the magical power to do good. Together they faced the barbarous scene of destruction before them, the smoking ruins of the thatched houses, the small churches stark and black in the shadows of twilight—above all the strange assembly of fighting men who stared at them open-mouthed.

18
Children of the Deerstone

"We are the children of the Deerstone!" began Paud, in a voice shaky with trepidation. "We are the children of the Deerstone. I, Paud, have come here to be united with Luke even though we live eight hundred years apart in the real world. If you do not believe me, ask Maeldubh to tell you what he knows—that in a battle of wills with him this afternoon, I carried the king's son, Luke, to safety from where Maeldubh was holding him prisoner."

At this Maeldubh made as if to charge at Paud but Macdara grabbed him roughly and exploded at him, "You worthless traitor, you swore you still had him secure in your keep." King Dermot, still wearing his disguise of a monk's robe but with the hood now fearlessly thrown back to show his true identity, advanced a few steps closer to the base of the stone. Maurice Regan and the king's soldiers followed in his wake, their hands clasped to the hilt of their short swords, their eyes watchful in the gathering dusk. Luke, distracted by the eerie call of a night-owl coming out to hunt on the shore of the lake, turned his head away from them in time to see the dark shadows of the masons as they came out of hiding behind the trees by the lakeside and cautiously inched forward to hear what Paud was saying.

"Maeldubh," continued Paud, "also possesses the ancient power of the stone-carver but he has used it only for evil purposes. Even now he has flung Malachi, the master mason, into a place they call the Shadow World, where he is neither dead nor alive. Before you all, I shall make Malachi come forth and prove to you all that I am who I say I am."

"How can he do such a thing?" sneered a voice. "It's impossible. This is just a trap laid to fool simple minds."

"Silence!" thundered the voice of the king. "In the name of Christ the King, Our Lord, hold your silence. If we are called to witness strange and unparalleled occurrences beyond our understanding and imagining, let us hold our tongues and keep our wits sharp about us."

Before he had finished speaking, the wind suddenly flared up, fanning the dying flames of the burning thatches and casting Paud and Luke in an amber pool of light. Paud closed his eyes and wished hard. "I wish for Malachi to come."

"No, no, he cannot do this."

A roar like you might expect from a great beast from ages past rent the air. Maeldubh had broken away from the grasp of the chieftain Macdara and hurtled towards the Deerstone, scattering all who stood in his way, his battle-axe raised above his head poised to strike at Paud. Luke screamed. At the same moment Dermot spun around to face the attacker, drawing out his sword as he did so. There was a resounding crash as sword and axe collided. Macdara's men did not wait for any further signal but threw themselves once again into battle, Paud and Luke for the moment forgotten...

But the spell of the Deerstone had not forsaken Paud. He felt himself drifting back alone into the Shadow World, until he hung suspended above the glassy black waters of the lake, upon which floated the reflection of a new crescent moon.

"Paud, Paud, is that you?" a hoarse whisper echoed down the valley.

"Malachi?" he answered. "You must come back with me now. Macdara and Maeldubh have attacked Glendalough." Paud could feel Malachi's presence near him, a presence as comforting as the regular breathing of his cat asleep on his bed in the dark, but he could not see where he was.

"Malachi," he called again quietly and immediately the call was taken up by a chorus of urgent echoes.

Except that they were not echoes of his own cry but the shouts of the first people to see Malachi step out of the shadows and walk towards Paud and Luke at the Deerstone.

As soon as he heard the first shouts of Malachi's name, Maeldubh broke away from his struggle with the king, and launched himself towards his rival Malachi, wide-eyed and roaring, "Damn you to Hell, Malachi, you will not have the better of me."

Paud and Luke jumped down from the stones and scrambled towards the river bank as the mason bore down on them. Malachi stood his ground, unarmed and fearless, for he had seen the chief Macdara load his sling and aim for the back of Maeldubh's head. His aim was deadly accurate: the mason slumped unconscious to the ground. Macdara wasted not a moment longer. He shouted a command and threw both his axe and sling to his feet. One by one his men followed his example, dismounting from their horses and falling to their knees.

Paud and Luke, crouching out of sight beneath the bridge, could hear nothing but the dull rhythmic thud as the weapons hit the ground. For several minutes no-one dared move or utter a word. The night air was still charged with the tension of the battle but while the mysterious appearance of Malachi remained unexplained, Dermot's men could no more celebrate their triumph than Macdara's could feel humiliation at having put down their weapons.

All eyes turned towards the massive figure of the king who stood alone at the bridge surveying the party of exhausted fighting men, but it was not the king who broke the silence but chief Macdara.

"King Dermot, it is said in our laws that 'He is not a king who has not hostages in fetters.' Let it be so. I, Macdara, of the line of the O'Tooles, humbly offer myself and these men to you as hostages in recognition of your overlordship of these lands and of all Leinster. From this day forward I am your servant to do your bidding.

"I cannot know who this strange boy is," he went on, "nor how he comes to carry the lost chalice of my great-grandfather Murchad. Neither can I know if he is as he says from another time but I fear these ancient powers, be they in the hands of Malachi or Maeldubh. Tonight we have all seen a strange sight here when Malachi walked out of the shadows at his bidding. Maeldubh lies beaten. It is enough for me to know that these powers are stronger in the hands of those who fight for you."

The king walked forward to Macdara and held out his hand. "I accept your tribute but I shall take no hostages. We are both men of Leinster—let us not be like fleas forever drawing blood upon each other's back. Together we can stand stronger against our enemies from without. Let your kinsmen unite under my rule and make this province of Leinster the strongest and wealthiest in the land. I shall take no prisoners except one." He waved contemptuously at Maeldubh who was already being bound in fetters by Captain Donnell. "Nor shall I condemn to exile any man who swears obedience to me today.

"Rather, let you all hear this, the word of a king: I have long ago put away all hatred of the O'Tooles. Have I not married Mór, of the O'Toole dynasty? Have I not made Laurence O'Toole abbot of Glendalough and sent my beloved son to live in your midst? Accept my dominion, come under my protection and you have nothing to fear from Dermot Mac Murrough.

"This holy city, which has seen such bloodshed and destruction, has a better way. Let Brother Laurence and his monks continue with their church-building and their prayers—we shall leave their city and the valley of the two lakes in peace."

"My lord Dermot," said Maurice Regan, coming forward, "the battle is over. It is almost nightfall. May we have your order to summon the monks from the priory and to deal with the wounded soldiers?"

"Of course, of course," replied the king, "and make ready the guest-house. Bring parchment and ink and ale too, for in the Book of Lecan it is said that it is one of the five lucky things of the king of the Leinstermen to drink the ale of Cualu. So Macdara and I, even at this late hour, shall drink the ale and sign our names to a document of peace. Call Laurence and Brendan and Malachi as witnesses."

"And the boys?" asked Maurice, nodding in the direction of Paud and Luke who were sitting in earnest conversation with Malachi around the hollow lower stone of the Deerstone. "What are we to do with them?"

"Bring them here to me."

Paud and Luke and Malachi walked together across the bridge at the king's command. (They shuddered with relief as they passed by the still unconscious figure of Maeldubh who was being hoist onto a makeshift stretcher and carried off by two of Dermot's soldiers.)

Night had now enveloped the valley but the sky was lit by a canopy of bright stars and the crescent moon lying on its back. The bells of the churches began to ring out in joyous peals signifying that the battle was over and that all the monks could come out from hiding to rejoin the community.

King Dermot extended his arms to embrace the two boys.

"Paud," he said, "we have heard now the story of your first visit to Glendalough and how you met my son Luke. We have also heard how you came across the mason Maeldubh hiding the chalice he had stolen and of your bravery in returning to the valley to give it back. For this, we thank you. We also thank you for the rescue of my son Luke from his captors and for saving the life of our master mason Malachi, whose work at the priory we hope will inspire generations to come. Your power is a mysterious one, and a frightening one, but by your mediation you have brought about peace in the valley of the two lakes.

"I want you to bring something away from here, and it is only right that that gift should be the chalice that has already crossed the boundaries of time and visited your city. We give you the chalice of Murchad and wish you god speed on your journey back to your own people and your own time for it is only right that you should leave us now."

Paud put out his hands to accept the chalice which Malachi had been holding. He was, it was true, anxious to leave but he was also overwhelmed with sympathy for this wild place and its epic people, and his eyes filled with tears.

"There is something I must do before Paud leaves us for the last time," said Malachi. "He and Luke unlocked the ancient power of the Deerstone with which my predecessor endowed it all those years ago in the time of St Kevin. In doing so, they have secured peace here in the valley of the two lakes, but they also unwittingly unleashed the darker side of the magic of the stones too. So, as Cronan did, I too shall use my power as a master-carver of stone, but this time I shall remove the spell. We thank and praise Paud and send him back on his wondrous journey to his own age. Then once he has gone, I ask Brother Laurence to bless the stones so that the mystery of the Deerstone's power may wither and pass away as all ancient things must."

It was time to go. The king, who had now thrown off his borrowed monk's robe and once more wore the magnificent white embroidered cloak, led the way towards the Deerstone with Malachi, Paud, Luke, Maurice Regan and a group of stone-masons in procession behind him. Approaching from the old Green Road from the priory came an excited group of monks led by the king's daughter Aoife and Brother Laurence O'Toole. Together they formed a wide circle around the stones. Paud stood on the hollow bowl of the Deerstone. There was perfect silence but for the water of the tiny river rippling over the stones and the eerie cries of the hunting owls calling to one another over the banks of the lake. Paud pulled off his wrist-watch, reached down and put it in Luke's hand. "Good-bye," he said. "Remember me as I will always remember you, my twin of the Deerstone."

He closed his eyes and summoned up the dark wondrous spell to transport him away. When he opened his eyes again, the little city of Glendalough was lying in ruins before him beneath the same crescent moon. In the distance he could hear the cries of the search

party who were still looking for him, but only a few feet
away from him was a lone fallow deer who had come to
drink at the bank of the river looking back at him with
startled amber eyes.

Epilogue

The chalice of Murchad O'Toole, or the Glendalough chalice as it came to be known, has become one of the most valuable treasures of the National Museum where it can still be seen today. The experts pronounced it one of the finest examples of ninth-century Celtic art which only goes to show how wrong experts can be for, as Paud knew, it was almost certainly made in the eleventh century, or about a hundred years before he had found it in 1162—but, of course, no-one would have believed him if he had told them the true story. He sometimes likes to go to the museum and look at it and Mick, the museum attendant, often takes it out of its glass case and lets him hold it.

"And, do you know something?" Mick tells people, "the boy takes it in his hands and says, 'Look' in the saddest voice you ever heard, as if he was mourning something he had lost, like, instead of having found treasure."

But of course we know that Paud is not saying, "Look." He is remembering Luke, his twin of the Deerstone, from whom he is now forever separated by the chasm of hundreds of years and whom he may never meet again.